The Snow Queen

D1566805

The Snow Queen

Eileen Kernaghan

THISTLEDOWN PRESS

©2000, Eileen Kernaghan
Second Printing 2003, Third printing 2004, Fourth printing 2007
All rights reserved

No part of this publication may be reproduced or transmitted in any form or by any means, graphic, electronic or mechanical, including photocopying, recording, or any information storage and retrieval system, without permission in writing from the publisher or a licence from The Canadian Copyright Licensing Agency (Accesss Copyright). For an Access Copyright licence, visit www.accesscopyright.ca or call toll free to 1-800-893-5777.

Library and Archives Canada Cataloguing in Publication

Kernaghan, Eileen
The snow queen

ISBN 10: 1-894345-14-2
ISBN 13: 978-1-894345-14-9

I. Title.
PS8571.E695S56 2000   C813'.54   C00-920061-4
PZ7.K45785Sn 2000

Cover illustration "The Russian Princess" by Charles Robinson
from *The Happy Prince and Other Tales* (Duckworth & Co. 1913)
Used with permission.

Cover and book design by J. Forrie
Printed and bound in Canada

Thistledown Press Ltd.
633 Main Street
Saskatoon, Saskatchewan, S7H 0J8
www.thistledownpress.com

Canada Council   Conseil des Arts
for the Arts   du Canada

SASKATCHEWAN
ARTS BOARD

Canadian   Patrimoine
Heritage   canadien

We acknowledge the support of the Canada Council for the Arts, the Saskatchewan Arts Board, and the Government of Canada through the Book Publishing Industry Development Program for our publishing program.

ACKNOWLEDGEMENTS

The song fragments in Chapter Twenty are loosely
borrowed from W. F. Kirby's translation of the *Kalevala*
(*Kalevala: The Land of Heroes*, Vol. 2, Dent: London,
Everyman's Library, 1st ed. 1907).

An earlier version of *The Snow Queen* appeared in
short form as "The Robber-Maiden's Story", in the
Canadian speculative magazine *TransVersions*.

for Gavin

Moon, free me, sun, let me out,
Great Bear, ever guide
(me) out of strange doors,
alien gates,
from this small nest,
from cramped dwellings!
　　　　　　　　— Elias Lönnrot,
　　　　　　　　New Kalevala

seventeen runes have I written
on hazel staves
and river stones
on apple boughs
and dragon bones
on sword and shield
on wagon wheels
and sleigh traces
on wolf's claw
and bear's paw
on serpent's tongue
on brooch and ring
on the night owl's wing
on silver, on glass, on gold
seventeen runes
for birth, for death
written on fire
and the wind's breath
and the eighteenth rune
which save in the hidden speech of love
is never told.

PROLOGUE

Looking back, years afterwards, she thought she could name the day, the hour — almost the exact moment — when things began to go wrong.

It was late in the afternoon, on a cloudless Sunday in July. The two of them, still in their church-going clothes, were perched high up above the street, in the narrow roof-garden their two households shared. The roses, flourishing in the hot weather, had shot up in their pots to form prickly head-high arches.

As usual Kai was reading a book. Holding it up against the slanting sunlight, he shielded his eyes with his free hand and squinted at the pages.

Gerda found the perfect rhyme she needed to finish her new poem, and penned the line tidily in her notebook: " . . . and sweet as the scent of roses on the summer air." She'd been working on it all week, in odd moments, worrying away at it to get the meter right. She read it through again from the beginning, and gave a small "hah!" of satisfaction. Kai glanced sideways at her.

"May I read you my poem?"

Kai closed his book, his finger marking the place. "Right now?"

"I'm sorry," said Gerda, confused by the gruffness in his voice. How impatient he sounded! She had always shared her poems with Kai. Always before he had seemed eager to hear them.

"No, it's all right. Go ahead. Is it very long?"

Gerda shook her head.

"Then read." His thin, dark face was turned toward her. The sun, glancing off his spectacles, hid the expression in his eyes.

She read the poem aloud, but all the joy had gone out of it. She spoke flatly, tonelessly, her voice draining the energy from her painstakingly crafted lines.

"It's all right," Kai said, turning back to his book.

"What's wrong with it?" she asked. Though she really meant, "What's wrong with you?"

"Nothing's wrong with it. It's fine. Quite good, in fact. But really, it's just another poem about roses. And sunshine. And love. It isn't as if you've said anything new about them, is it?"

"You always liked my poems. You *said* you did."

"But I'm older now. If you must know, I've found there are things in this world that matter more than pretty verses about rose-gardens."

When had her oldest playmate, her dearest friend, turned into this harsh-tongued stranger? "Things that matter more than love?" she asked, dismayed.

He gave her a look of pity and condescension. "*This* matters," he said, and he thrust his book at her. She glanced down at the open page. It was covered with symbols, formulae, equations. They might as well have been magical runes, for all that she could understand them.

"Mathematics, Gerda. Calculus." He took the book out of her hands, gestured to others in the pile beside him. "Physics. Chemistry. That's what matters to me, Gerda. Not poems."

"I write about what is beautiful," she said.

"That's because you're still a child."

"Sixteen in August," she reminded him in a small, faint voice.

"As I said. A child. As you get older, you come to see things more clearly." He plucked a rose from the nearest pot. "See this? Black spots all over the leaves. The petals brown and fading. Ugliness. Decay. Why write poems about things that are only pretty for a week? Now *this* . . . " He showed her a sheet of foolscap, the page covered with equations — or perhaps, she thought, it was one single, sprawling equation. "This is beautiful. Elegant. Real. This endures."

The marks on the page were blurred, suddenly, by Gerda's tears. "How hurtful you are," she said. "How cruel."

Kai looked at her in honest bewilderment. "Why do you say that? How can it be cruel, to explain what should be self-evident?"

But she had already gathered up her petticoats and skirts, and with inelegant haste was clambering through the window into the refuge of her bedroom. She refused to let Kai see her cry.

Chapter One

The drumming had started again. It throbbed in the thick, stale air of her father's hall, pulsed in her flesh like a second heartbeat. Ritva knew it would go on all night. How she loathed the whole business — the monotonous drumming, the writhing and shaking and frothing at the mouth. She hated the sight of her mother lying in the mud, a limp heap of deerskin and feathers, emptied like a husk. She hated how tired and wrung-out her mother looked afterwards, and how foul-tempered she was, when her soul at last returned to her exhausted body. Most of all she hated the reminder that one day this power, and this dreadful obligation, would be hers.

"They can't make me do this," Ritva promised herself. "I will be a hunter instead. Or a reindeer herder." Squirming down into her nest of musty skins, she stuffed her fingers into her ears.

By morning the drums had stopped. Ritva lay still for a long time, her eyes crusted with sleep and smoke, staring up into the blackened rafters of the Great Hall. All she could hear was the soft cooing of the pigeons, the crackle of burning logs, the rasping snores of her father's men, still sprawled in drunken slumber beside the hearth. After a while she crawled out of bed, pulled on her tunic and leggings, laced up her deerskin boots. Then she felt under her pillow for her hunting knife in its embroidered sheath. This last year or so she had begun to sleep

13

with it close to hand. She fastened it to her belt, and wandered over to the hearth in search of breakfast.

Ritva's mother had taken off her shaman's garments and had put on instead a skirt and a long-sleeved, high-necked bodice. Ritva's father had stolen them years ago from a lady of high rank who had been foolish enough to travel through their part of the forest. The black velvet skirt was frayed at the hem and rubbed shiny at the seat. There were gravy stains on the silk bodice, half the jet beads had come unstitched, and there was a gaping rent under one arm. In her shaman's robes Ritva's mother possessed a frightening dignity, but this tattered, grubby finery diminished her. When she took off her robes she took off her strength, her authority, her ability to inspire fear.

Her eyes were rimmed with red and her face looked pinched and sallow, drained of blood. The chin-whiskers she had recently begun to sprout were more noticeable than usual. "High time you were up," she said, giving the rabbit on the spit an irritable poke. "Look at this place. It's a pig sty. A proper daughter would have been up at first light, sweeping and scrubbing."

"Then you should find yourself a proper daughter, shouldn't you?" said Ritva nastily. "It's no business of mine, to clean up after a lot of drunken swine."

"Nor mine either. There was no rest for me last night." Ritva's mother dipped a ladle into the soup cauldron and sucked up a noisy mouthful of broth. "Old Lars will live. The spirits have given back his soul. But every time it gets harder. I'm too old for soul-journeying, Ritva. It makes my bones ache." An edge of self-pity sharpened her voice. "I should be sitting by the fire with my embroidery in my lap."

Ritva smirked at the idea of her mother doing embroidery.

"Where are you off to?" It was a peevish, old woman's question.

Ritva shrugged. "How should I know? Maybe I'll go hunting. Or maybe I'll ride out to the edge of the world, and never come back."

Her mother made a noise as though she had something caught in her throat. "You'll be lucky if that poor old bone-rack makes it out of camp, never mind the world's edge." Her voice rose, became thin and querulous. "And what will become of your kinfolk, if there is nobody to beat my shaman's drum when I am gone to my grave?"

"How tiresome you are," said Ritva, with an exaggerated yawn. "I'm sick of you always singing that same tune. Maybe I will keep riding forever." And she stomped across the stone floor, slippery with spilled beer and pigeon-dung, to the far end of the hall where her good old patient reindeer Ba was tethered.

Chapter Two

"My dear Mrs. Sorensen, it's a scandal, what's happening to our weather." Fragrant steam curled up as Gerda's mother poured coffee into her best rose-patterned cups. "The coldest January in a hundred years, they say."

The tall porcelain stove in the Jensen's parlour radiated heat. The room, with its thick hangings and dark mahogany furniture, smelled cozily of beeswax and potpourri and fresh-baked bread.

Gerda blew on the frosted windowpane and rubbed a clear patch so that she could look out. Behind the green velvet curtains lay a still white world, locked fast in ice. Already, in mid-afternoon, it was growing dark. These days, few townsfolk ventured out. The cold snatched away your breath, made your lungs ache. She thought of stories she had heard, of the far northern lands where the air itself froze, and everywhere you walked, your shape remained behind like a snow-angel or a ghost.

"And how is your house guest enjoying this weather?" Gerda's mother was asking Mrs. Sorensen. "A cousin of yours, I believe?"

"Actually, it seems she's a sort of second cousin, on my husband's side." Kai's mother was a pleasant enough woman, but inclined to be vague. "She comes from some outlandish northern country — Antarctica, I think she said — so of course this weather suits her perfectly."

"Oh, surely not Antarctica," said Mrs. Jensen. She had been a governess in her youth, and had some grasp of geography. "You must mean Iceland. But I didn't know you had connections so far north."

"My dear, no more did we. But Madame Aurore wrote Mr. Sorensen such a charming letter, to say she would be passing through on her way to Copenhagen, and could she come to call. So of course we invited her to stay with us. She is *such* an interesting young lady, and terribly clever."

"Your Kai seems very taken with her," Mrs. Jensen remarked.

"Oh, indeed. He's quite the scholar, our Kai, and she knows about all those scholarly things — the way the two of them go on, about algebra and philosophy and such, it puts my poor head in a spin!"

"I declare, I've forgotten the ginger-cake," said Mrs. Jensen. "Speaking of having your head in a spin . . . "

"I'll get it," said Gerda, turning away from the window. She hurried through the kitchen into the spice-scented larder and lifted down the tin. With one ear on the murmur of conversation behind her, she cut thin slices of cake and arranged them on a china plate.

"Your Gerda is growing into quite a beauty," she heard Mrs. Sorensen say in her high, clear voice. "When I think what a tomboy she used to be . . . "

Gerda snatched up the plate and went to listen behind the half-open door.

"Tomboy indeed," said Gerda's mother. "Hair always in a tangle, boots muddied up to the ankle, petticoats a-draggle, racing after your Kai."

"How they do change," said Mrs. Sorensen, a trifle wistfully. "My Kai is such a sober-sides now, you'd never think what devilment he used to get up to, falling out of trees, letting the Larsens' pigs out of their pen . . . they were two of a kind, he and Gerda, like sister and brother, and scarcely a jot of sense between them. But your Gerda, I can see she's turned into a proper young lady . . . "

"When she chooses to be," said Gerda's mother. "But she's as headstrong as ever — always acts before she thinks, her father says. And lately she's taken to writing poetry . . . which is all very well, I suppose, but I wish she could darn stockings as tidily as she makes rhymes!"

Gerda's cheeks flamed. Was this how her mother saw her — headstrong, thoughtless, a draggle-hemmed hoyden? And Kai — now that he was so grown up and serious-minded, did he think she was still the same wild girl who had climbed trees with him, and fallen into streams, and shredded her stockings clambering through bramble hedges? If only she could learn to be pale, and elegant, and mysterious, like the Sorensen's lady visitor. Then perhaps Kai would see her as somebody worthy of his attention.

"Gerda, my dear, have you fallen asleep in there?" Her mother's voice was half-amused, half-impatient. Gerda straightened her morning-cap and smoothed her kerchief. She drew herself up as tall as she could and swept into the parlour with what she hoped was an air of ladylike composure.

"And of course you'll both be going to the Kristoffersen's winter soiree?" said Mrs. Sorensen, accepting a slice of gingercake.

"Of course," said Gerda's mother.

"Of course," echoed Gerda, practising a cool, mysterious smile.

❖❖❖

"You'll never guess what our dear Madame Aurore let slip to Kai — it seems that her late husband was a Baron. My dear, imagine it!" Mrs. Sorensen waved her ostrich feather fan so emphatically that her bonnet ribbons danced.

"Well, you must admit, she dresses like a Baroness," said Gerda's mother.

"Indeed, such gowns, such furs, such jewels . . . how could I have not guessed she was of noble rank? What an honour for our house!"

Just then their hostess Mrs. Kristoffersen, the Mayor's wife, bore down on them, imposing in emerald green taffeta.

"My dear Mrs. Jensen, how lovely to see you. And you, Mrs. Sorensen. And you've brought along your charming house guest — you *will* introduce me, won't you?"

"With the greatest of pleasure," said Mrs. Sorensen.

"What a lovely gown she's wearing," said Mrs. Kristoffersen, sounding faintly dubious. "But don't you think it's a little . . . "

"Elaborate? Perhaps a little. But it's the festive season, after all. And my dear, I do think we are far too provincial here."

"Actually, I meant a little youthful-looking, for a woman of her age."

"Oh, but she's really quite young," said Mrs Sorensen. "It's just that she's been widowed, and of course that would make one look more . . . mature."

"How curious," said Mrs. Kristoffersen. "I'd have taken her for thirty, if she was a day."

Gerda hung back in the shadows, glowering at the tall woman in the ice-blue damask gown. An hour ago, setting out for the Mayor's house in her new lace-flounced dress of mulberry-coloured velvet, with her hair done up in a mass of yellow ringlets, her heart had raced with anticipation. Kai would be at the soiree, and surely he would dance with her. Kai always danced with her. They would grow flushed and breathless in the quadrille, and when they waltzed together he would whisper silly riddles in her ear. They would go in to supper together, and make jokes about the other guests, and the coolness of these past months would be forgotten. But Kai had not spoken to her all evening. Instead, he had danced attendance on the Sorensen's visiting cousin as though she were the Queen of Iceland.

She's much too old for him, thought Gerda spitefully. *Thirty if she's a day.*

But what did age matter, if you were were tall and slim and elegant, if you skimmed across the floor in your Paris gown like a beautiful blue-feathered swan? Above the wide bell of her skirt Madame Aurore's waist was slender as a girl's, her shoulders, bared by her low-cut bodice, marble-white. The glittery threads woven into the blue damask sparkled like ice-crystals under the chandeliers. Her hair, the pale white-gold of winter sunlight, swooped modishly over her ears and was caught up at the back with a diamond clasp.

And now the musicians had struck up a waltz and Kai was leading this woman out onto the dance floor while Gerda lurked morosely behind a potted palm: hating her new gown, which — she now decided — made her look twelve years old, and fat, hating her straw-coloured corkscrew ringlets, her round cheeks and rosy complexion. I'm too short, she thought despairingly; too healthy-looking; and worst of all, too young.

Gerda's throat felt tight; there was a prickling behind her eyes. She slipped quietly into the cloakroom, where she stood among the fur overcoats and boots, dabbing at her cheeks with her pocket handkerchief. Through the cloakroom window she could see fresh snow falling.

CHAPTER THREE

Ritva rode into the pinewoods that girdled her father's camp. Ba's reins hung slack; the old reindeer knew the way to Ritva's secret place as well as she knew it herself.

In the crotch of a tree, at the edge of a shadowy clearing, someone had long ago wedged a bear skull. The skull faced the sunrise. Its weatherworn surfaces made a glimmering white patch against the dark wall of pines.

Ritva dismounted, laid a handful of dried cranberries at the foot of the tree as an offering. Then she stood with Ba's reins gathered into one hand and remarked to the bear skull, "I *hate* this place."

"This place?" the skull asked, sounding a little aggrieved.

"No, not this place. I mean my father's hall. I am sick of stepping in spilled beer and vomit. I am sick of always having to sleep with a knife under my head. And most of all I am sick of my mother."

"And what has your mother done to offend you now?" asked the skull, in its sombre, deliberating way.

"The same as always. She spits, and slobbers, and has fits, and falls on the ground in a trance. She is a horrible old woman, and I hate her."

"She is a shaman," the skull reminded her. "She is not responsible for what she does when the spirits possess her."

"And this is what I will become? A foul-tempered, drooling old hag?"

"You are her daughter. Her power is in you also."

"When did I ask to inherit her power? I don't want it. I want to live by myself in a hut by the river. I want to ride south, to where it's always summer."

The skull said, "Child, you may not turn your back on the gift the great god Aijo has given you. Nor on the obligations birth has placed upon you."

"I didn't ask for his gift. Come to that, I didn't ask to be born."

"No," the skull agreed sadly. "Nobody asks to be born. Nor do most of us ask to die. Those are things the gods decide. And their gifts are not easy to refuse."

Chapter Four

O n sunny mornings the roofs and chimney pots seemed wrapped in spangled cotton batting. The meadows beyond the town were covered with a glittering white crust, as hard as pavement. Even the Sound was frozen over, so that if you wished you could walk all the way to Sweden. The river was crowded with skaters, scarved, capped and mittened, their breath smoking on the crystal air.

Gerda had been to church that morning in her new fur-trimmed bonnet and her garnet-coloured mantle with the velvet collar. Still dressed in her Sunday finery, she asked leave to go skating; her mother, preoccupied with luncheon preparations, nodded absent-minded permission. Minutes later Gerda and her friend Katrine — hands tucked in quilted muffs, shawls and mantles billowing — were gliding sedately over the ice.

"What has become of Kai?" asked Katrine. "I never see you together."

"What he does is no business of mine," said Gerda. She had meant to sound offhand, but the sharpness of her voice betrayed her. Katrine looked round, surprised.

"But you've always been such good friends . . . "

"Perhaps, when we were children. But now he thinks only of his studies, and we have nothing to say to one another."

"Boys never say anything interesting, anyway," observed Katrine, with the superior wisdom of seventeen.

They skated on, around the bend of the river. The sharp air stung their cheeks, brought tears to their eyes.

Sleighbells jangled just ahead and they steered closer to the bank, under leafless elder-branches.

Silver harness trappings gleamed. All along the river skaters wheeled in slow circles, staring, as the sleigh swept by. The team was a matched pair, white as milk. The woman who grasped the reins so carelessly in her pearl-trimmed gloves had hair the colour of winter sunlight.

"That's *her*," breathed Katrine. "Kai's cousin from the north."

"She *says* she's a cousin," said Gerda. "I don't think they know a single thing about her."

"She's very beautiful," observed Katrine.

"I suppose," said Gerda, grudgingly.

"She looks like a princess," said Katrine, admiring the woman's ermine-lined cashmere cloak, the silver-blonde hair streaming artlessly over her thrown-back hood. "Her husband, or her father, must be someone very important."

But Gerda could not imagine this elegant, free-spirited creature as someone's daughter, still less as someone's wife. She seemed to exist outside the bounds of domesticity, answerable to no one but herself.

A little way downriver the white sleigh glided to a stop. Gerda watched the woman lean down from her seat, laughing. And then she reached out a white-gloved hand to draw someone, a young man, up beside her.

Gerda put her mittened hand over her mouth to smother a cry. She could not see the young man's face. At this distance the dark shaggy head in its knitted cap, the narrow back in its nondescript woollen coat, could have belonged to anyone. Yet

Gerda knew, with a sick emptiness in her breast, that the boy beside the pale-haired woman was Kai.

Gerda had spent the morning shopping. When she arrived home, breathless and parcel-laden, she found Kai waiting. He made a great pretence of stamping snow from his boots on his own doorstep, but she knew he had been watching for her. She stepped into her front hall, set her parcels down on a bench, and looked warily at Kai through the open doorway.

"Come in," she said. "Before I let all the heat out."

He nodded absently, and stepped over the sill.

"Let me take your coat."

He shook his head. "I'll not stay. I only came to tell you . . . "

Gerda waited, slowly unwinding her scarf, unfastening her mantle, taking off her bonnet. Under all her layers of flannel vests and chemise and stays her heart was thudding against her ribs. She knew, before the words were out, what Kai was going to say.

"Gerda, I'm going away for a while."

"With her?"

"If you mean the Lady Aurore, yes, with her. She's invited me to return with her to her winter home in Sweden. She lives in a great house near Uppsala, where the university is."

"Kai, you can't be serious! To travel all the way across Sweden, in the dead of winter . . . "

"Why not? The winter roads are nothing to her. She says that blizzards are her natural element."

"But Kai, who *is* this woman? What do you know about her?"

"I know that she is a woman of great learning — a Doctor of Philosophy. Learned men come from many countries, to talk with her and consult her library, in which there are many thousands of volumes, on every subject under the sun. Even the philosopher Sören Kierkegaard has been to visit her. She is writing a book of her own, in which she hopes to reveal the secret pattern of the universe. And Gerda, this is the best part, I have not told you this — she has asked me to be her pupil— her assistant! When this great work is finished, my name could be written with hers!"

What had become of her quick-witted irreverent Kai, who made her laugh with his clever nonsense? When had he turned into this humourless young man who spoke in the lecturing tones of a schoolmaster? "And when will this great work be finished?" she asked in a small, sad voice.

"Oh, not for years, perhaps for decades," Kai told her. "Such works are not written in a day."

She saw that his thin face was flushed, as though with fever. His eyes, which all these past months had seemed so cold and distant, burned with a hectic light.

"But surely your mother and father will not give you their permission, to go so far from home?"

"Gerda, do you imagine they would stand in the way of such an opportunity? They are not rich, you know — I was to become a lawyer, or a schoolmaster. It was not what I wanted, but I thought I would have to make my own way in the world."

"I will never see you again."

"Of course you will see me again, you goose. I will come home in the summertime, and we will sit under the rosebushes, and I will tell you of all the marvellous things I have seen, and read about."

But they were the words of a patient adult humouring a sulky child, and she took no comfort in them.

What could she say to him? She could not tell him how often she had dawdled behind the others on the way home from church, hoping that he would catch up, and walk beside her. She could not say that when she and Katrine chattered over their embroidery — furnishing imaginary parlours, rocking their some-day babes in imaginary cradles — it was Kai's thin, solemn face she saw bent over a book beside the fire. You could not say such things to a young man, even one you had known since you were a toddler at your mother's knee.

"And what news of Kai, Mrs. Sorensen?" The late afternoon sun fell in a dazzle through freshly-washed windows, pooling like molten gold on Mrs. Jensen's best embroidered cloth. Gerda froze in the act of taking Mrs. Sorensen's empty coffee cup. The cup rattled on its saucer, and she set it down.

"My dear Mrs. Jensen, I wish I *had* news to tell you. We are getting quite anxious, there has been no letter these two months past. I did not even hear from him on my birthday. I know how busy he must be with his studies, but surely, a note to let us know when we are to expect him home . . . "

"But you *are* expecting him home?"

"Oh, most certainly. That was always the agreement. But still, one does grow a trifle uneasy, when one hears nothing . . . "

Her voice trailed off.

Mrs. Jensen's glance met Gerda's. Her eyes were troubled. She had always had an uncanny knack for reading her daughter's thoughts. But the look was a fleeting one, and she turned away at once to reassure Mrs. Sorensen. "My dear, I am sure you will hear any day now. They are all so thoughtless, these young folk, so wrapped up in their own affairs . . . now try one of these cakes, it's a new recipe — and do let Gerda refill your cup."

"I'm sure you're right," said Mrs. Sorensen. "If he had fallen ill, or had an accident, his benefactress would certainly have informed us."

But Gerda, like Mrs. Jensen, had seen how tired and anxious Kai's mother looked, had observed the dark, sleepless circles under her eyes.

The spring drew on. The plum trees blossomed, and then the lilacs. The beechwoods burst into pale new leaf. Before long it would be midsummer, and the sun would rise three hours after midnight. For Gerda, all this loveliness seemed wasted. She was sick at heart, wondering what had become of Kai.

"If only we could travel to Sweden, and find him," Mrs. Sorensen wailed to Gerda's mother. "But Mr. Sorensen is not well, the trip would be too much for him, even if we could afford to close the shop . . . with the business so slow these days, one must think of where one's next meal is coming from . . . "

"You will have to do without me this spring," announced Katrine. "I have had an invitation from my cousins, in Copenhagen, to stay with them for the end of the Season."

"For how long?" asked Gerda, despairing.

"Two whole months," said Katrine. "Just imagine! All of the spring season in Copenhagen . . . They are so lively, my cousins. My mother says they attract young men like moths to the flame. There will be no end of balls and soirees . . . and picnics in the fine weather. Oh, Gerda, what a shame you won't be there as well!"

"How lucky you are," said Gerda. But she was imagining the dreariness of the months to come, with Kai's absence always on her mind, dulling her spirits, and no blithe Katrine to distract her.

Seduced by the Baroness Aurore's airs and graces, her Paris gowns, the title in front of her name, the village would hear no word against her. And if Kai had vanished from their lives — if he had not even sent a letter for his mother's birthday — well, was it so strange that a young man, immersed in his studies and caught up in the excitement of the great world, should forget to write?

What could Gerda say or do that would shake them from their complacency? *Next month, next year, in his own good time*, they said. Kai would return to them with a gentleman's manners and a sheaf of diplomas in his trunk.

But Gerda knew in her heart that by then it would be too late.

Awake at midnight in the silent house, Gerda stared out at the full moon riding high above the beechwoods. Was Kai watching that same moon through the branches of the pines in some northern forest? *Sweden*, she thought. *Kai is in Sweden*. How impossibly far away that seemed — yet those were Swedish lights that twinkled just across the narrow waters of the Sound.

In spite of all obstacles, all objections, Gerda knew what she must do.

"Katrine, I'm going to ask you to do something for me. If you will do this one thing, I will never ask for a favour again."

"Gladly, if I can," said Katrine, unsuspecting. "Shall I buy you a French bonnet in Copenhagen?"

"No, nothing like that. I want you to write me a letter."

"Don't be silly, of course I shall write you a letter. We're not all like Kai, you know."

Gerda shook her head. "No, listen to me. I want you to write me a letter, inviting me to stay with you for a fortnight in Copenhagen."

Katrine's blonde eyebrows drew together. Her wide, pale brow wrinkled. "But Gerda, how can I do that? I am a guest myself, I could not be so presumptuous — "

Gerda seized Katrine's two hands. "Hear me out, dearest Kat. I don't really mean to stay with you. But I must show my mother the invitation."

"Gerda!" cried Katrine, her eyes widening. Half in horror, half in delight, she exclaimed, "You can't mean it! You wouldn't dare!"

"Why not? You know the Sorensens can't go to look for Kai, though they're half out of their minds with worry. You know how they are, they're embarrassed to make a fuss, so they've convinced themselves Kai can come to no harm. But who is this woman, this Baroness Aurore? Is she really a Baroness? Is she even a relation? Do you know what I think, Kat? I think she has placed a spell on Kai, and will not let him come home."

"But how will you find him?"

"I told Kai's mother I wished to write to him, and she has given me his address."

"But to set off alone, on such a journey — Gerda, it is unthinkable!"

"Why do you say so? By all accounts, Sweden is a civilized country. Are you not travelling alone, to visit your cousins?"

"But I am only going to Copenhagen, not off into the wilderness, and my cousins will send their carriage for me. Besides, my parents will know where I am!"

"I have a little egg money saved up — I too will hire a carriage. And my parents will know where *I* am — or at least, they will think they know. All you must do, dear Kat, is to write the letter. Is it so much to ask? I will say my prayers, never fear — God will watch out for me. And as soon as I have found Kai, I will send word."

CHAPTER FIVE

Ritva fought her way slowly out of sleep. Dream images clung to the edges of her mind like scraps of mist.

Her stomach felt queasy, her clenched neck and shoulder muscles ached, and there was a dull throbbing behind her eyes. Even her bones hurt. As she struggled to sit up, a pain between her ribs, sharp and unexpected as a knife thrust, made her cry out.

"It's about time you woke up."

Ritva rubbed sleep out of her eyes. Her mother was standing at the end of her bed, holding a skinning knife.

"Go away," said Ritva, lying back and covering her eyes with her forearm. "I'm sick."

"Ah," said her mother, sounding pleased. "Another dream?"

Ritva grunted.

"They're coming closer," her mother observed, with evident satisfaction. "And what happened this time?"

None of your business, old woman, Ritva was tempted to say. Instead, she rolled over and turned her face to the wall.

"Oh, we're sulking today, are we?" Ritva felt a foot poke her sharply in the middle of her back.

She sat up, cursing, and met her mother's dark, impassive stare.

"You know well enough what happens," Ritva said. "You dreamed the same dreams, once. Why must I live through it all again?"

"No dream is the same as any other dream," her mother said. "And how am I to guide you, unless I know what paths you walk?"

"Listen, then, old woman," said Ritva, "for I'll not tell it twice." She drew a shallow, painful breath and began.

"In my dream I had been travelling for many days over marsh and tundra, and through forests of birch and pine. At last I came to the edge of an icebound sea. On the shore stood a great grey stone, which spoke to me out of a mouth filled with bear's teeth. 'I am the earth's holding stone,' it said. 'I hold down the fields, so that they will not blow away in the wind.' Then a creature like an ermine came to me, and said that he was my guide. He led me to a cave in the side of a mountain. All over the walls and roof and floor of the cave were mirrors, and in the middle of the cave a fire burned, so that it was like standing inside the sun."

"Was there more?" her mother asked impatiently.

Ritva nodded.

"Well?"

"On the fire was a cauldron that seemed as big as half the earth, and beside it stood a giant working a bellows. I knew at once that I was going to die." She shuddered, remembering what came next. "And then the man cut off my head, and chopped my body to pieces, and dropped everything into the cauldron. Afterwards he threw my fleshless bones into a river, and when they floated to the surface, he pulled them out, and flesh grew on them again. It was horrible," she cried out. " I felt every stroke of the axe. I felt the scalding heat of the cauldron, the icy cold of the river-bottom. I knew what it was to die by iron, and fire, and water."

"Yes," said Ritva's mother. "I remember that dream. There will be worse to come."

CHAPTER SIX

On the morning of her departure, Gerda came down to breakfast in her plainest grey wool gown, her soberest bonnet, her sturdiest buttoned boots. The small wooden crucifix her grandmother had given her hung from a ribbon at her throat.

"Dear me," said Mrs. Jensen, looking askance at her daughter's costume, "you're as drab as a churchmouse today. What a dull family Katrine's cousins will think us!"

"The roads will be dusty," said Gerda, helping herself to bacon omelette. "Don't worry, I've packed my best dress in my portmanteau."

She had assured her mother that Katrine's uncle would meet the stagecoach when she arrived in Copenhagen; but that, like so much else she had told her family this past week, was pure invention. When she reached Copenhagen she meant, instead, to take a room for the night at a respectable hostelry, rising before dawn to catch an early morning coach to Elsinore. If anyone should inquire why a young unmarried girl was travelling unaccompanied, she had her answer ready. "I am a governess," she would explain, "on my way to take up my duties in a Swedish household." Perhaps if she kept her distance, and discouraged conversation, no one would ask.

➤➤➤

The carriage rattled northward from Copenhagen along the rough coast road, past red-tiled wayside inns and fishermen's huts. The sea wind, blowing in through the open windows, smelled of brine, and kelp, and rotting fish.

In the harbour at Elsinore Gerda boarded a ferry and crossed the narrow Sound to Sweden. The sea was quiet that day, the crossing uneventful. She stepped onto the pier at Helsingborg with a sense of relief at the miles she had already put behind her. She tried not to think of the distances that lay ahead.

She was excited, and astonished, and appalled, at what she had done. But now, standing in the cold grey daylight on the wharf at Helsingborg, in the shadow of the Keep, sudden panic seized her. She was in a strange town, in a country whose language and customs she barely understood. She had come too far, there was no possibility of turning back; and now she must find her own way, uninvited, unexpected, on unknown roads to a stranger's house. Her excitement faded, leaving behind a sick anxiety.

In one of the streets running back from the harbour she came upon a tavern, but it was filled with seamen shouting in a dozen foreign tongues, and she was afraid to go in. Finally a woman of the town noticed her hovering uncertainly in the courtyard.

"Lost, dearie?" the woman called out.

Gathering up her skirts and her portmanteau, Gerda picked her way across the cobbles. The woman, who was tall and very blonde, looked down at her with amusement.

"Can you tell me where I can find lodgings, and a carriage for hire? I must leave in the morning for Gothenburg."

"There's an inn next street over," said the woman. "And as to the stables, just follow your nose. Ask for Nels, the ostler, and tell him Annie sent you."

➜➜➜

Exhausted after the rough, dusty journey from Helsingborg, Gerda spent that night under yet another strange roof, in yet another unfamiliar city. In the morning she set out by canal boat along the great waterway that crosses Sweden, winding through rivers and lakes and series of locks like flights of stairs. Holiday-makers, business travellers, and dozens of chattering small children thronged the deck. Gerda mingled with the crowd in comfortable anonymity. Through the long sunlit days and evenings they glided through green corridors of birch and elm, past tidy stone-walled farmhouses, ancient castles, Viking burial mounds. Once Gerda would have delighted in the journey; now all she felt was a desperate impatience to reach the east coast, and Kai.

Beyond Stockholm, beyond Uppsala, Gerda's hired carriage jounced along a narrow forest track. Now and again it emerged from between black walls of pines into open meadowland, strewn with lichen-speckled boulders. The day was warm and damp, the sky overcast, and by late afternoon a thin rain had begun to drizzle through the trees.

The coachman reined up before the tall iron gates that marked the entrance to the Baroness Aurore's estate. On either side crouched improbable stone beasts, fanged jaws wide and roaring, talons clutching their stone pedestals, wings uplifted as though they were about to take flight. A chill wind had come up as the light faded, and now the rain was sweeping down in wide grey sheets.

A bronze bell, green with verdigris, hung in a kind of wooden cage atop a post. The coachman pulled the bell-rope, and presently the gates creaked open.

"There's no one here," said the gatekeeper, peering out.

Gerda thrust her head through the window of the coach. The wind snatched at her bonnet; rain stung her cheeks. The horses whickered and stamped their feet.

"What do you mean, no one," she shrieked over the rising wind. "Isn't this the house of the Baroness Aurore?"

"Indeed it is, Miss. But the Baroness has already left, this week past, to summer in the north."

"And her assistant? Is he not here?"

The gatekeeper had already begun to close the gates. "You mean the young man?" he called out through the gap that remained.

"Yes, yes," cried Gerda. Her throat was tight with panic. "Please, where has he gone?"

"North with the Baroness," said the gatekeeper, and the gates swung shut.

The coachman's boy got down from his seat and opened the carriage door. "My master says, where to now, Miss?"

Gerda stared at him. Her heart rattled against her ribs.

The Baroness was gone, and Kai with her, the house abandoned. What would become of her now? She had not thought past this moment.

"Miss?"

She tried to answer him, and choked on a sob.

"Don't you have anywhere else to stay?" He was a pleasant-faced boy, about her own age, and seemed concerned.

Wretchedly, she shook her head.

"Should we take you back to the city?"

"I haven't enough money left," she whispered, ashamed.

"Well, we can't leave you here," said the boy, and he called up to the coachman, "What shall we do with this young lady, sir? It seems she has nowhere else to go."

Now the coachman himself was looking in at her. "What, no family in these parts? No one who will take you in?"

Gerda bit down on her lower lip to stop it quivering. Her eyes were blurred with tears, and her nose was starting to run.

"Well, this is a fine how do you do," said the coachman. He was rotund, red-cheeked, fatherly looking. "But I'll tell you what. My old auntie lives round here, and she'll put you up for the night."

"How kind you are," said Gerda, remembering her manners.

"Well now, we can't leave a young lady like you on the side of the road, can we?" He patted her awkwardly on the hand. "My auntie will give you a good supper and a warm bed. Things will look cheerier in the morning. They always do."

The coachman's aunt lived in a pleasant thatch-roofed cottage. A river ran near her front door: behind were open fields and an apple orchard. The windows were made of stained glass, glowing squares of cherry-red and cobalt blue. A fire blazed in an open hearth. There was smell of coffee brewing, and fresh-baked bread.

The aunt was tall and broad, with mild grey eyes behind thick spectacles, and grey-blonde hair braided round her head.

She peered down at Gerda, benignly disapproving.

"Well, Miss, I can't imagine what your parents were thinking of, sending you off alone into these Godforsaken parts, with no money and no one waiting at the other end. Don't they know that these high-born folk change their houses the way they change their Sunday hats?"

"I believe," said Gerda, fighting back fresh tears, "there must have been some misunderstanding about the dates."

"So it would seem," said the coachman's aunt. "Are they always as absent-minded as this, your parents?"

"Certainly not," said Gerda. "They are sensible, church-going folk, and I'm sure if my mother were not so busy with all my younger brothers and sisters, she would never have got the dates mixed up."

"Is she a relation of yours, the Baroness?" asked the coachman's aunt.

"A second cousin," said Gerda. "On my mother's side."

How easily the lies came, thought Gerda, once the first one is told.

"Well, perhaps I shouldn't be saying this, since she's a connection of yours — but I've always been one to speak my mind. That Baroness of yours seemed to me a proud, unfriendly kind of woman, with a cold look in her eye. I don't know that she'd have made good company for a lively young girl like yourself."

"You've seen her, then?"

"Oh many a time, when she's driven by my cottage, or passed me on the road."

Gerda dared not ask the one question she desperately wanted answered: *Was she alone? Was there a young man with her?*

Instead she said, without much conviction, "My mother has always spoken well of the Baroness."

"I have no doubt. Folks always speak well of their relatives, if they have a title in front of their name. Well, that's neither here nor there, is it? We must think what to do next."

"I will write my family a letter," said Gerda, "and they will send me money to pay for my keep, and for my journey home."

"They needn't trouble themselves about paying me," said the coachman's aunt. "I'm glad of a bit of company, if you want the truth. But yes, you must write them for ticket money, straight away. I'll see that my nephew posts it." And she bustled off to her parlour to look for paper and ink.

41

Chapter Seven

The old woman came to Ritva in the dead of night, wearing a shaman's robe and carrying a painted drum. Her face was scored and furrowed, burned by the sun and the arctic wind to the colour of dead leaves. Her long hair was grey as ash. She grinned, showing toothless gums, and Ritva cried out, not in fear, but in sudden recognition. This was her grandmother Maija, her mother's mother, who had died when Ritva was three.

Ritva knew the old woman's story. It was Ritva's story too. When Maija's only daughter became pregnant by a blonde outsider, a bandit-chief, Maija left the tents of her Saami people and followed her daughter to the bandit's camp. The women of the camp remembered old Maija, still, with admiration. Like all the women of her line, she possessed the shaman's gift. But in the soul of Ritva's mother there was too much passion, too much heat, and her power had curdled like spoiled milk. The power in Maija was like the northern lights — clear and beautiful and without heat.

"Do not be afraid," said Ritva's grandmother, who had been dead these fifteen years. "I have come to teach you a song."

And she began to beat on her drum, and chant in a cracked and quavering old woman's voice.

Who is the hero who will do battle with the Woman of the North?
Who is the shaman who will break the spell
of the Terrible Enchantress,
Drowner of Heroes and Devourer of Men,
she who is mistress of the Dark Land
beyond the Cave of the North Wind
where earth and day end.
Storm and fog and ice
and the cold of eternal darkness
are her weapons.
She has torn the sun and the moon from the sky
and has hidden them away
in the heart of the stone mountain.
Who is the hero who will journey to her kingdom?
Who is the shaman who can overcome her power?

The drum fell silent, the words of the song trailed away like wisps of smoke. Ritva was alone. But a faint, half-remembered odour lingered in the darkness near her bed — a smell of bog myrtle and reindeer moss and healing herbs.

CHAPTER EIGHT

My dearest Kat,

I know you will be relieved to hear that I am safely arrived in Sweden. I have taken lodgings with a most respectable woman, and you need have no fears on my behalf — but I pray you, do not tell my family, for of course they believe that I am with you in Copenhagen!

Forgive me, dear Kat, I must ask you for yet another great favour. I have enclosed a letter to my family, to be sent from Copenhagen — will you be so kind as to post it for me? My mother frets when I am an hour out of her sight. I wish to reassure her, as I hope I am reassuring you. I know you will understand that until I find Kai, and bring him safely home with me, I must resort to these schemes and subterfuges. There will (I hope) be a reply from my family, sent to your address. I will write to you again, and tell you where it may be forwarded.

I trust you are having a splendid time, dear Kat. I'm sure that all your dance cards are full, and that you have won the heart of every eligible young man in Copenhagen.

With fondest love,
Your Gerda

Dearest mother and father,

I have quite fallen in love with Copenhagen! I have seen all the notable sights, and visited more parks and museums than I can count on two hands. You will be surprised, on my return, at how knowledgeable I have become! The shops are quite splendid, and we have been to . . . imagine it! . . . two balls already! I am so grateful that you allowed me to visit here with Kat. I should not have wished to miss such an opportunity!

I wonder, though, if you might be able to send me a little more spending money? I cannot believe how expensive things are in the city, and how quickly boots and slippers wear out when you are walking all day, and dancing half the night! Also, Kat and I have been invited (such excitement!) to a very grand affair, hosted, I gather, by people of the highest Copenhagen society. My best gown, which seemed quite suitable at home, appears — I have to confess it — just a jot provincial amongst all these Paris frocks.

Gerda read what she had just written with shame, and dismay, and a terrible foreboding. To so wickedly deceive her parents, to abuse the trust of her dearest friend . . . and worst of all, to discover how easily these lies slipped from her pen! Could any end justify such unforgivable means? And yet what choice did she have? Having come so far, she could not turn back. Kai must be found.

"Here is my letter." She sealed it, and wrote the address of Katrine's Copenhagen relatives in a careful hand. Then she gave it to the coachman's aunt. "Will you see that it is sent as soon as possible?"

"Of course," the woman said. "But it will be some time before you have your reply. You must make yourself at home, my dear. Why don't you go out into the garden and enjoy the sunshine? I love this time of year, when the pear tree is in bloom, and all the daffodils out."

Gerda sat with her morning coffee in the little walled garden. Drifts of grape hyacinths and narcissi made bright patches of blue and yellow among the mossy paving stones. In a sun-drenched corner the first rosebuds were beginning to swell.

The sight of them brought a lump into Gerda's throat. Would she ever again sit with Kai among the rose bushes on their sunny roof?

She wandered back into the kitchen, where the coachman's aunt, arms floured up to the elbows, was kneading bread.

"The Baroness Aurore . . . " Gerda said hesitantly. "Do you know where she has her summer home?"

The coachman's aunt looked round at her. She swiped her perspiring brow with the back of a floury hand.

"Oh, hundred of miles to the north, they say, beyond the pine forests, in the land of the reindeer herders. Though why anyone would choose to live in such a cold, inhospitable place I can't imagine."

Her gaze narrowed. "Why ever do you ask, child? Surely you're not thinking of going there?"

"Of course not," said Gerda. "I only wondered where she had gone."

"Best to get yourself home as quick as you can, child," said the coachman's aunt, giving the dough an emphatic punch. "Much as I enjoy the company, your family must be missing you sorely."

"Yes," Gerda murmured. "Yes, I suppose they must." She felt a sudden spasm of guilt, sharp as a cramp in the belly.

The coachman helped himself to the coffee pot, and a large slice of the apple-cake his aunt had just set out to cool on the window ledge. He sat down in the big armchair by the stove, and put his feet up on a needlepoint footstool.

"Happened to hear some news in town today," he remarked through a mouthful of apple-cake.

"Oh yes?" said his aunt, wiping her hands on her apron and pouring herself a cup of coffee. She sat down in the chair opposite, leaning forward expectantly.

"The lady from the big house, the Baroness . . . "

Gerda put down her book. The coachman looked across the room at her. "You were asking where she goes, summers?"

Gerda nodded wordlessly. Her heart was thudding. She felt short of breath.

"Seems she goes way up into Norrland. She has a big house on the Torne River, north of a place called Vappa-Vara. Reason I know, I picked up a missionary at the harbour, off a northern ship. He'd just come back from taking the good word to the reindeer-folk who live in those wild parts. We got to talking, and he told me stories about this beautiful, rich, fair-haired woman who had built a great house at the edge of the pine forest. The reindeer folk are mortally afraid of her, it seems — they think she is some sort of witch, or sorceress."

"Well now, I never heard *that* particular thing said about her," observed the coachman's aunt, appreciatively. "Why do you suppose they would think such a thing?"

"Well, you must remember, these are poor godless folk, full of all kinds of heathen notions. And a beautiful woman like that, choosing to live all alone in a great house in the midst of the wilds — why, it would be an odd thing if they did *not* think she was a witch."

"Well now, Miss Gerda," said the coachman, "I have found out what you wanted to know, for what good it will do you. And I wouldn't say no to another cup of coffee, if you would be so kind."

"How late it is," said the coachman's aunt, yawning.

"Are you not ready for bed, child?"

"In a little," Gerda replied. "May I borrow a book from the shelf?"

"Why, my dear, help yourself. They are my son's books; I'm not much of a reader myself. But he'll not begrudge you the use of them, I'm sure."

Gerda waited until she was sure that the coachman's aunt had blown out her candle and settled into her feather bed. Then she crept to the shelf and took down the heavy, gold-stamped atlas. Sprawled on her stomach on the hearth rug, she opened it to Mercator's map of northern Europe.

A country without roads, without cities. On the west, uncharted mountain wastes; on the east, a jagged coastline plunging into the icy northern seas. In between, a land of rivers, moors and marshlands, and trackless pine forest going on to the world's edge. How could she hope to survive in such a wilderness? And what hope had she of finding Kai?

She shivered and hugged herself. Then she put the book back on its shelf, lit a candle, and made her way to bed.

Chapter Nine

Ritva sat up in bed and saw her dead grandmother crouched in a corner under the pigeon-roosts.

"I have come to tell you a story," her grandmother said. "It is a story from the old times, before the southerners came. A boy went to the shaman's tent, and asked how he too could learn to be wise.

"'If you would be wise,' said the shaman, 'you must travel north to the shores of the frozen sea, where the world ends. When you return, you must tell me what you have learned.'

"After forty days and forty nights the boy returned.

"'What have you learned?' the shaman asked.

"'That ice is white.'

"'Only that?' said the shaman. 'You must go back.' And so the boy travelled again for forty days and forty nights, to the edge of the world and back.

"'What have you learned this time?' the shaman asked.

"'That ice is cold.'

"'Go back,' said the shaman. 'You have more to learn.'

"The shaman waited for forty days and forty nights, but this time the boy did not return, for he had travelled too far and remained too long, and had frozen into a pillar of ice. And the shaman knew that the boy had found wisdom at last; for he had learned that ice is death."

Chapter Ten

The money arrived, along with a cheerful, gossipy letter from Gerda's mother. Gerda packed up her few possessions in her portmanteau and prepared to take her leave. When the coachman came to drive Gerda to Uppsala, his aunt set out an enormous breakfast of porridge, bacon, eggs and buns. She saw Gerda off in a flurry of kisses, and cautions, and tears, and good advice.

On the stagecoach north from Uppsala Gerda's carriage-mate was a small plump woman of sixty or so, with bright dark eyes and grey hair drawn back in a knot. In her plain dove-grey gown with pearl buttons up to the chin, she reminded Gerda of nothing so much as a pouter pigeon.

The woman tucked a bulging carpet bag into a corner, settled herself into her seat, and turned briskly to Gerda. "And where are you off to all on your own, my dear?"

"To visit a friend," said Gerda. She supposed it was near enough to the truth.

"Oh yes? And where does your friend live?"

"Oh, a long way off. In Norrland, somewhere on the Torne River, near a place called Vappa-Vara . . ."

"Indeed! I know it well. That's all the way into Saamiland, where the reindeer people live. Well, you will have your adventures, my dear, before you get to Vappa-Vara. It's late in the year to be setting out on a trip like that. You'll be running into the autumn storms soon, and the nights closing in."

Gerda looked at the woman with interest. "You've travelled in Norrland?"

"Oh, indeed I have, many a time, and a long way north of that. Ingeborg Eriksson is my name — I dare say you've heard of my books. I was a great one for travelling, in my time — though with my rheumatics, I'm getting past those overland trips."

"Did you go by yourself?"

"Oh yes — it's best, I think. At first I took along a lady companion — my family thought it was unsuitable for a young woman to travel alone. But my companions always seemed to fall ill a week or so into the journey . . . you have no idea how inconvenient that can be! My dear, may I offer you some advice?"

"Of course."

"When you're travelling in those parts, you must be sure to pack your own provisions. I can't emphasize that too much. It simply doesn't do to depend on the hostelry along the way. A little salt fish, that's the best you can hope for, and the bread always seems to be mouldy."

"What sort of provisions?" asked Gerda.

"Plum pudding," Madame Eriksson said firmly.

"Plum pudding?" asked Gerda, disconcerted.

"Exactly. You can't go wrong with plum pudding. I used to take forty pounds of it, on my longer journeys. It keeps well, and there's nothing more nourishing."

"And what else?"

"What else? Let me see." The woman began to tick things off on her gloved fingers, beginning with her thumb. "Lamp wicks. You can't have too many of those; you simply can't get

51

them out in the wilds. Candles, of course. Plenty of candles. And as to clothing — vests, drawers, petticoats, all of wool; eiderdown is best for your coat. Make sure it has a fur collar you can pull up, and sleeves long enough to cover your hands. In the cold weather I would wear a sheepskin over that, and finally a coat of reindeer skin. In those climes the last spring frost comes in the middle of June, and the first one of winter arrives before the end of August."

What a sight you must have looked, thought Gerda, imagining this plump little person in her three thick coats, one on top of the other.

"Not to mention two pairs of thick stockings," Madame Eriksson went on. By now she was on the fingers of the second hand. "Felt boots — the kind that come up over the knee. A fur-lined cap, and a few rugs and shawls won't come amiss."

"I should never be able to afford to buy all those things," sighed Gerda.

"Then," said her companion, "you'd do best to cut your visit short. Once the snows come, and the northern nights set in, you will find you need every bit of that, and more." She rummaged in her bag, brought out a bottle of red wine and a loaf of black bread. "And in the summer, of course, you'll do well not to be eaten alive."

"By wolves?" asked Gerda, alarmed.

"By mosquitoes. You can run away from wolves. From the mosquitoes, there is no possibility of escape. Well, now, my dear," she said, breaking off a piece of the bread and offering it to Gerda, "we have a good long trip ahead of us. Suppose you tell me what sends you off into the northern lands."

As the carriage rattled over the stones Gerda chewed on her crust, sipped wine straight from the bottle, and told her story.

The wine was making her too sleepy to think of lies, and it seemed to her that this grandmotherly woman, with her kind, uncritical gaze, could be trusted with the simple truth.

"Well," said Madame Eriksson, when Gerda had finished, "I must say, I admire your enterprise. Though I've never yet met a man worth going to the ends of the earth for." She looked at Gerda with kindly cynicism. "Ah yes, my girl, I see it in your eyes. You think this Kai of yours is different. Well, you're young, you're entitled to your illusions." She held out her hand for the wine bottle. "I worry about you, though, traipsing off on your own into the wilderness, when you're unaccustomed to travel."

"I will manage," Gerda said, trying to keep her voice from trembling.

"I doubt it," the woman said. "No maps, no provisions, no money . . . "

"I have money," said Gerda.

"Oh, I dare say — but it won't be enough. Listen," the woman said, "if I were ten years younger, I would be tempted to come with you. As it is — I have a friend who might be persuaded to help. This adventure of yours is just mad enough to appeal to her."

"Help me? How?"

"Well, let's think what you need. Good advice, for a start. But then if you were one to listen to advice, you would not have come as far as you have. I expect the princess could easily spare a carriage and some warmer clothes. I propose that the two of us pay her a visit."

"She's not really a princess, is she?"

"Oh, every bit of it, her blood is as blue as my magnesia bottle. She's a princess in her own right, in a nice little southern kingdom whose name I've forgotten. Married beneath her, you might say, for her husband is only a count . . . why, what's the matter with you, child, your eyes are as big as dinner plates."

"I've never met a princess," wailed Gerda, aghast. "I wouldn't know what to say to her. I wouldn't know how to behave."

"Nonsense," said Madam. "A more down-to-earth, common-sense sort of princess you'd never hope to meet. If you're going to make a habit of travelling, my girl, you'll learn to get along with people of all sorts, from peasants to princes. And what's more you'll learn to sleep wherever you put your head down, whether it's a skin tent, or a goat hut, or a royal palace."

"Yes, ma'am," said Gerda, chastened. Madame Eriksson drew a book out of her bag and settled back in her seat to read. Gerda rode the rest of the way in anxious silence, wondering if she would be expected to curtsy. Whatever would the ladies of her village say, if they knew that Gerda Jensen had been entertained by royalty?

The princess sent her landau to the hostelry at Gavle to collect them. They drove through birch groves, and pine woods, and down a long avenue of lime trees, at the end of which stood a copper-roofed manor house surrounded by terraced formal gardens. On either side of the granite-pillared portico, rows of mullioned windows were set in an imposing red-brick facade.

A maid in starched cap and apron greeted them. "The princess will see you in her drawing room," she said. She led them through a high-ceilinged entry hall hung with shadowy tapestries, past rows of bronze sculptures on marble plinths, and along a carpeted corridor. In the drawing room there were crystal chandeliers, tall mirrors in gold-leaf frames, solemn portraits of ancestors in old-fashioned clothes, vases of flowers, an elegant green-tiled stove, and airy white curtains caught up in swags and festoons. At the far end of the room French doors stood open, with a view of green lawns and rose gardens.

"My dear Ingeborg," said the princess, rising to greet them. "How splendid to see you!" She took hold of Madame Eriksson's hands and kissed her on both cheeks. "How well you look!" And she gave Gerda a wide, encouraging smile.

"This young person's name is Gerda Jensen," said Madame Eriksson. "She is a young woman of more courage than good sense, a quality one meets far too rarely these days."

"I'm inclined to agree," said the princess. "I am delighted to make your acquaintance, Gerda Jensen."

Gerda rose from her nervous curtsey, and looked shyly at her hostess. She was small, full-bosomed, tiny-waisted, olive-skinned. Clusters of glossy black curls nestled at her ears and the nape of her neck. Her eyes were a velvety brown, with thick black lashes, her cheeks flushed with good health and high spirits. Her gown was exquisite — simple of line, but made of a soft rose-coloured silk brocade. Little rose-pink slippers peeked out from under the hem.

"Will you both take a glass of wine?" asked this enchanting creature.

"With pleasure," said Madame Eriksson, sinking into a silk-upholstered armchair. And Gerda, who never until this day had drunk anything stronger than coffee, found herself sipping wine from a crystal goblet.

Just then a little girl of five or so, a miniature version of the princess in pink and white muslin, burst into the room. A small white dog leaped excitedly at her heels.

"Oh, *maman*," exclaimed the child, when she saw the two visitors, "it is the lady who was chased by wolves!"

"Odile, my poppet, I should never have told you that story," laughed Madame Eriksson, scooping the little girl into her capacious lap. "I'm sure I must have given you nightmares."

"Oh, no," the child assured her. "It was a wonderful story. My governess never tells me stories like that."

"I should hope she does *not!*" said Madame Eriksson. "But my dear Princess, I must confess I have come to beg a favour."

"Anything," said the princess, refilling her friend's glass, "if it is in my power."

"Have you a coach and driver you could spare for a week or so, do you think?"

"But of course . . . my dear, how exciting! Are you off on another one of your journeys?"

"Oh, I am not asking for myself. Not this time. No, it is for Gerda, who is sitting here so quietly and demurely, like the well-bred young lady she is. She has this wild scheme, you see, to go off into the northern lands in search of her friend, who has managed to become mislaid."

The princess turned to Gerda with lively interest. "All on your own? Surely not!" She glanced down at the dog, who was nosing his way into Madame Eriksson's open carpet bag. "Odile, for goodness sakes take that creature outside and amuse him."

"He smells my supper," said Madame Eriksson, amused.

"Your supper, indeed! I think we shall manage something better than that," said the princess. "But now, Gerda, you must tell me the whole story, before I die of unsatisfied curiosity. Here, give me your glass."

That evening Gerda dined on salmon pâté, and wild duck in madeira sauce, and cloudberry mousse. She ate alone at a little lacquered table in her bedchamber, for Madame Eriksson declared they were both too exhausted from their trip to be good company. The plates and tureens were willow-patterned Chinese porcelain, and the heavy silverware bore the princess's family crest. Gerda fell asleep beneath a swansdown counterpane, in a bed hung with rose-red silk damask. She did not wake until a maid in a stiff lace cap came in with her breakfast tray.

In the morning room the princess handed round pastries, and coffee in delicate chinoiserie cups. "My driver will take you north along the coast road to Lulea, and then on to Boden — it's a garrison town, and my nephew is an officer there. But beyond Boden is wilderness — two hundred miles of it, to Vappa-Vara. I don't suppose you ride?"

Gerda shook her head.

"No, I thought not. Well, I dare say you will have to travel by cart, then. You'll find it dreadfully uncomfortable." She looked at Madame Eriksson, who nodded in grim agreement. "Well, perhaps you can go part of the way by boat. I'm sure my nephew can arrange something. In the meantime, dear Ingeborg has stripped my cupboards of fur coats and hats and flannel petticoats. We shall have to find you a trunk for them all."

The princess, and Madame Eriksson, and the child Odile, and two parlour maids and the white dog all crowded behind Gerda on the manor house steps as the coach-and-four pulled up. The carriage was lavishly gilt-embellished, and had the princess's coat of arms on its door.

"I have drawn you a map of the road to Vappa-Vara," said Madame Eriksson, "and perhaps you would like to put this book in your portmanteau. It's one of mine — I've taken the liberty of signing it for you."

"May God be with you, my brave Gerda," said the princess. "You must promise me, if you ever need help, you will send me a message."

"I promise," called Gerda through the carriage window.

"Did you pack those pairs of flannel drawers?" Madame Ericksson shouted out, indelicately.

"Every one," cried Gerda. They all went on waving and calling out advice as the coachman rattled the reins, the coachman's boy leaped up beside him, and the coach moved off. Gerda peeked curiously into the enormous picnic basket the cook had packed for her, then settled back with a sigh into the velvet cushions.

North of Uppsala, it was never entirely dark, nor entirely light. There was mile after mile of pine forest, and then the trees thinned, and they came to a desolate country of swamps and tangled, stunted birch trees, with snow still lying in patches on the ground. Near Boden, under a leaden sky, the road once again disappeared into forest, with mist hanging low in the branches.

But inside the gilded coach, Gerda had rabbit skins to rest her feet on, and cashmere shawls to wrap around her shoulders. As the weather grew colder, she put on the ermine-trimmed hat the princess had given her, and thrust her hands into the princess's grey squirrel-skin muff.

By now she had grown used to the creaking and jouncing of the coach over the rough forest road. She dug through her basket of provisions for fruit and butter-rolls, then, weary of watching the endless grey miles slide by, fell into a comfortable doze.

She was dreaming that she had found Kai, and that they were sitting together in the princess's coach, on their way to the princess's manor. Kai's arm was around her; she could feel his warm breath stirring her hair. "Thank heavens you came for me, my brave Gerda," he was whispering. "I knew one day you would rescue me from that woman's vile ensorcelment."

And suddenly, in her dream, the coach lurched to a spine-jolting stop. Her sleep was shattered by a confusion of sounds — loud male voices, the shrill whinnying of the horses, the coachman shouting.

Someone wrenched open the door of the carriage, seized Gerda and dragged her to the ground. Her captor smelled of sweat, and musty skins, and woodsmoke. She could not scream; a large dirty hand was clapped over her mouth.

"Let her go," a voice said, in heavily accented Swedish: a self-assured, commanding female voice.

Hastily released, Gerda staggered. She reached out for the door handle, clung to it for support.

The bandit who had seized Gerda sidestepped out of the way as a young woman strode forward. She was an inch or two taller than Gerda, and in her leather shirt and breeches looked as strong and broad-shouldered as a man. Her lank black hair hung raggedly to her shoulders. She had a bone-handled hunting knife stuck through her belt.

Gerda shrank against the carriage. Close at hand she heard a shrill, surprised cry, abruptly cut short.

She looked into the robber-girl's black, mocking eyes. Her stomach twisted with cramp. Her throat had seized up so that it was hard to get her breath.

The robber-girl's strong brown hand closed around Gerda's wrist and squeezed hard, grinding the bones together. She put her foot on the wheel and climbed onto the coachman's seat, dragging Gerda up beside her. Then she gathered the reins and cracked the whip with a flourish. Two bandits who had been holding the horses' heads jumped out of the way with grunts of surprise. The horses set off at a trot, and the carriage went careening along the rough track through the pinewoods. Behind her, Gerda could hear someone bellowing at them to stop.

CHAPTER ELEVEN

Ritva felt like a prince up there on the coachman's seat. On the floor by her feet was a wicker basket full of sausages and white bread. She concentrated on driving one-handed while she delved into the basket wih the other. Then, with her mouth full of sausage, she turned her attention to the girl.

She was dressed like a princess — or like Ritva imagined a princess must dress — in a fur-collared velvet coat and fur-lined boots of embroidered felt. "What are you going to give me for saving your life?" Ritva asked her in Finnish.

For answer the girl made a whimpering noise in her throat.

"Don't start blubbering," said Ritva, reaching for another sausage. "You'll ruin that coat."

The girl clutched her squirrel-skin muff to her chest and stared straight ahead over the rumps of the horses. Angry red blotches flared on her pale cheeks. Her mouth trembled.

"You can give me those boots," said Ritva, lapsing into her mother's Saami tongue. "And that muff." She spoke loudly and clearly but there was no response. Just then the wheels jolted over a root. Ritva shrugged, and concentrated on the road.

The coach creaked and shuddered its way over the rutted track, and after a while they came to Ritva's father's hall. It had been a castle once, a citadel of massive limestone blocks, but centuries of winter frosts had loosened the mortar and cracked the stones. Now there were great holes in the wall where ravens

61

nested, and the central tower was riven from top to bottom as though by a lightning bolt.

One of her father's men stood gawking as Ritva rattled up to the gate.

"Look after these horses," Ritva shouted, tossing him the reins as she jumped down from the driver's seat. "And see that nobody goes near this coach, or I'll slice up your liver for the soup." Ritva had peered inside the coach, had seen the quilted satin walls, the velvet seats, the rabbit furs strewn like snow-drifts on the floor. The surly band of cutthroats and deserters her father called his private army would quickly turn such luxury into splintered rubble.

She dragged the yellow-haired girl down from the coachman's seat and pushed her through the ruined castle's entranceway. As usual it was cluttered with skis, snowshoes, fishing gear, jumbled heaps of wolf and reindeer skins. A guard dog snarled and snapped at the girl, its growls subsiding into a whine when someone shouted at it.

The dim, cavernous hall was thick with smoke. One of the women sat over the low fire that smouldered in the middle of the stone floor. She was nursing her infant and stirring the soup-pot with a birchbark stick.

The girl coughed and put her hand over her nose. It occurred to Ritva that the place must stink, what with all the animals stabled inside, the heaps of pigeon-dung, the jumbled piles of half-cured skins and last week's bones, though she hardly noticed it herself.

Ritva motioned to the girl to sit down on a bench beside the fire, and ladled out some soup to warm her belly, with a crust of black bread to gnaw on. She watched with interest as the girl ate, sipping the soup so daintily that not a drop spilled down her chin, breaking off bits of bread and slipping them into her mouth, and afterwards wiping her lips and fingers on a lacy handkerchief.

"What's that you've got there?" Ritva's mother had crept noiselessly up behind them.

"None of your business," said Ritva, not turning round. "Go away, old woman."

"That's no way to speak to your mother." The shaman pinched Ritva's earlobe between thumb and forefinger and gave it a sharp tug. Ritva slapped the hand away.

"She's a plump little thing," remarked Ritva's mother.

Ritva glanced round suspiciously. "Why do you say that, old witch? Are you planning to boil her up for your dinner?"

"Plenty of meat on those bones," observed her mother, with a gap-toothed grin.

"You're a horrible old woman," said Ritva, "and you're not getting your hands on her."

"And what do you mean to do with her?"

"I don't know yet. But I had to rescue her from my father — he'd have cut her throat for the sake of her coat and muff."

Ritva stalked to the fire, where the girl was hunched over her stew. "What's your name?" she asked gruffly, in Finnish.

The girl looked up. Her blue eyes were wide and bewildered.

"What do they call you?" Ritva prompted her with a sharp finger in the midsection.

Still no answer.

She's an imbecile, decided Ritva, with a pang of disappointment. Then she thought, *maybe she just comes from some southern country, where they speak a different tongue.*

She pointed to her chest. "Ritva," she said. She levelled a grimy forefinger at the girl, and raised her brows.

"G-g-gerda," the girl responded, stuttering with fright.

Not an imbecile after all, thought Ritva. *What a splendid pet she will make, this little white rabbit. If anyone tries to come near her, I will stick my knife in their ribs.*

It was growing late, though evening light still seeped through the chinks in the wall. The women built up the fire, setting a big grease-encrusted cauldron of soup to boil, and spitting a brace of hares. Thick smoke curled along the blackened rafters, seeking a way out. Then the men of the camp returned, stamping and cursing, and shouting to the women to bring them food.

Ritva took Gerda by the arm and pulled her into the shadowy corner under the pigeon-lathes that she had long since claimed for her own. All the pigeons stirred in their sleep and began to coo as Ritva walked under their perches, and her old reindeer Ba nuzzled the girl with his cold nose. Ritva tickled him with her knife until he backed off.

She took a straw-broom and swept away the day's accumulation of pigeon-droppings, threw down some fresh straw, and spread out her bed of musty skins.

She pulled Gerda down beside her on the straw. The girl sat hugging herself, as still as a hare run to earth by wolves. Only her eyes moved, darting anxiously from Ritva to the immense, echoing, firelit space behind her. Ritva drew her knife from her belt and thrust it under the rolled up rabbit skin she used for a pillow. She liked to keep it handy, just in case.

Some of her father's men had broken into loud, drunken song. Gerda shivered, and turned her head away. Her teeth had begun to chatter. "Lie down," said Ritva. "They won't bother us here. Go to sleep."

The girl squirmed down as far as she could in the bed. Every muscle was tensed, her breathing fast and shallow. Ritva lay awake for a long time, conscious of the small, rigid, motionless shape beside her.

"What use is she?" snapped Ritva's mother. "Look at her hands — she's never done a stroke of work in her life. I mean to let Ivar's son Henrik have her. He needs a wife, and he seems to have taken a fancy to her, though what he sees in such a pasty-faced, washed-out creature I cannot guess."

Ritva imagined Gerda in fat, foul-mouthed Henrik's embrace. She felt sick at the thought of it. "You will *not*," she said.

Grimacingly horribly, Ritva's mother waved her skinning knife. "Shall I slice off those ears, stupid girl, that will not listen to good sense? Shall I cut out your wicked tongue, that dares to say no to your mother?"

"Not if I can help it," retorted Ritva, stepping out of reach.

"You don't care about this girl," said her mother, abruptly changing her tactics. "You do this to make me angry. In everything, you defy me. Never have I had a minute's joy of you, since the evil day I bore you."

"Nor I you," said Ritva, unrepentant.

"Can she cook?" asked her mother.

"What, now you'll make a hearth-slave of her?"

"Why not? Or is she too feeble even to stir a kettle, or fetch an armload of wood?"

"What a ridiculous old woman you are," said Ritva. "This girl comes to us riding in a gilded coach, dressed like the daughter of a king, and you would set her to stirring the stewpot? Clear your head of visions for a minute, Mother. Think what manner of people she must come from — and what they might pay to get her back."

Her mother's eyes narrowed. "You have not spoken to your father about this?"

"When did I ever speak to my father about anything?"

"Have your pet princess, then, if you must," said Ritva's mother. "Do with her as you will." Her voice was sullen, but Ritva had seen the flicker of greed in her face, not quickly enough concealed. "Talk to her. Find out what place she comes from. I will find her family."

"And how do you mean to do that?"

"I may be a stupid old woman, in your eyes, but I have my powers yet."

But Ritva knew that those powers were fast fading. Each time the healing trance or the journey of far-seeing left her mother more exhausted, as though the return from the spirit world became more arduous as the mind and body grew more frail. One day, Ritva thought, she will not return. And it will be through me that the spirits speak, my body that the spirits possess.

She thrust away those thoughts, for they weighed heavily upon her.

Chapter Twelve

"Here, eat," said Ritva. "You'll get as scrawny as my old reindeer." She ladled some porridge into a bowl and thrust it in front of Gerda.

Gerda's stomach twisted at the sight of the grey, slimy mess. She pushed away the dish and shook her head.

"Stupid thing, you have to eat. Why will you not eat?" Ritva reached out to put her hand on Gerda's forehead. "What's the matter? Are you sick?" After the first day or so she had given up on Finnish and now spoke to Gerda in a rough soldiers' Swedish picked up from her father's men.

"Not sick. Afraid," said Gerda.

"Afraid? Of what? Of those drunken louts?"

They sat in the midst of the wreckage caused by last night's feasting. One of the bandits still snored in front of the hearth with his head in a puddle of beer. The women calmly stepped over him to tend the fire and stir the porridge-pot.

"They won't dare lay a finger on you. They know if they do I'll stick my knife between their ribs."

"Not only them." Gerda shot a wordless glance towards Ritva's mother. The Saami woman was wearing her shaman's robe, decorated with magic signs and hung about with the skins of small animals. All that night, and all the day before, she had crouched in a dark corner of the hall, neither eating nor drinking, speaking to no one and glaring venomously at anyone who dared to approach. With a curved prong of reindeer horn she beat a slow monotonous rhythm on a round skin-covered drum.

"What, my old mother?" said Ritva. "She's all bluff, she won't harm you. Anyway, look at her, she hardly has a foot in this world anymore."

"What is she doing?" whispered Gerda.

"One of the men has the lung sickness. My mother's drum is a reindeer, and she is riding it to the Land of the Dead to ask for his soul back."

"Has she always been like that?"

"What, a shaman?"

"I meant, has she always been so . . . " Gerda groped for a tactful word, " . . . so uncivil?"

Ritva snorted. "Uncivil! Is that what you call it, in the south? If you want to know, she's an evil, disgusting old woman, and I hope that next time she goes into one of her trances, she never comes out."

"But she is your mother," said Gerda, appalled.

"So what if she is? Is that supposed to make me like her?"

"Perhaps," said Gerda, thinking about the wicked step-mothers in fairy tales, "she is not your real mother?"

Ritva threw back her head and gave a hoot of laughter. "Oh, she's my mother, right enough. Who else would have suckled a brat as horrible as me? But you haven't told me why you ran away from home. Did you have a mother like mine, who thumped your ears and pinched your nose and let you go hungry when you disobeyed her?"

Gerda had a sudden vision of a cozy, lamplit sitting room, smelling of beeswax polish and fresh-brewed coffee and pot-pourri. She imagined her mother's gentle, anxious face, bent over a lapful of knitting; the restless flicker of needles in her long slim fingers; the way her jaw would tense and her eyes widen at the sound of footsteps on the walk, the opening or closing of a door. Tears of guilt and homesickness welled up; her throat ached. She swiped her sleeve across her eyes. Not trusting herself to speak, she shook her head.

"So why did you run away?" It was a game for Ritva, this relentless questioning. She tormented Gerda with her curiosity, like a cat tormenting a mouse.

"I didn't," Gerda said. "My mother is not like yours. She is kind and good."

"But you left."

"Only because I had to find Kai."

"Then tell me about this Kai. Is he your brother?"

"No."

"Aha!" Ritva grinned at Gerda, her eyes mocking. "Your lover, then."

"No!" exclaimed Gerda. "He is my friend. Only that. I love him as a friend."

"Neither your brother nor your lover? And still you followed him into these wilds?"

"Wouldn't you search for your friend," asked Gerda, "if somone had put an evil spell on him, and stolen him away?"

"I don't have friends," replied Ritva. "My old reindeer, Ba — and the knife in my belt. Those are all the friends I need."

"How very lonely you must be," said Gerda. She spoke more with anger than with sympathy. *Truly, she is her mother's daughter*, Gerda thought — *spiteful and mean, caring for no one but herself.*

"I could never have come this far without the help of friends," said Gerda. She thought of dear, trusting Katrine, whose trust she had betrayed; of the coachman's aunt, of Madame Eriksson and the Swedish princess. And then, with anguish, she remembered the princess's two servants, who, but for Gerda, would still be alive and safe at home with their own families.

"Come and see Ba," said Ritva, suddenly jumping up as though bored with her game.

The reindeer was old, and so thin that his ribs showed.

"Don't you feed him?" Gerda asked.

"Of course I feed him. He's skinny because he's so old. But I love you dearly, don't I, you miserable old bone-rack?" So saying, Ritva tickled the reindeer under the chin with the point of her knife. The animal regarded her morosely, but did not move his head. Ritva put the knife away in her belt, and blew softly through pursed lips. The reindeer lowered his gaunt head and gently nuzzled Ritva's neck.

"See how he loves me, my old Ba? He would do anything for me. He would lie down and die for me, if I asked."

The poor thing looks ready to lie down and die in any event, thought Gerda, but was wise enough not to say so.

"But you —" Ritva swung round to stare at Gerda. Her eyes were bold and black under her heavy brows. "You say you love this Kai. Would you die for him, then?"

Gerda was about to reply, when it occurred to her that this wild girl might put her to the test. "He would not ask me to do that," she said cautiously.

"But if that's what it took, to save him?" Clearly, Ritva was enjoying this game. She stared at Gerda, unblinking, unrelenting.

Suddenly Gerda was furious. How dare she mock her for loving Kai? This coarse creature, whose only notion of love was to hurt and torment?

"Yes," she said, defiantly meeting Ritva's gaze. "If that's what it took, I would die for him. Have I not already proven that, following him to the ends of the earth?"

At this, Ritva made a rude noise. "The ends of the earth! What could *you* know about the ends of the earth?" And she stamped off across the straw-littered floor, raising a cloud of dust and flies. Gerda met Ba's doleful, eloquent gaze. She had the uneasy feeling that the conversation had not been about Kai, or herself, or the reindeer, at all.

Ritva tossed sleeplessly in the white summer night. Finally she pushed herself up on one elbow and stared down at Gerda. "So how *did* you get here, anyway?" No response. She prodded Gerda sharply in the ribs, and heard her squeal with surprise.

"Talk to me."

"What should I talk about?"

"Tell me how you came to be riding in a coach with a coat of arms, out here in the middle of no place. There has to be a story in that."

"There is," Gerda said. "A long one."

Someone howled a curse at the far end of the hall. A bench fell over, and then a table. Bottles smashed.

"Then why not tell it," said Ritva. "We've got all night."

Chapter Thirteen

At last Gerda came to the end of her tale. Ritva yawned and lay back, staring up into the rafters.

"All these people who gave you food and shelter, loaned you their coaches — what did you have to give them in return?"

Half-asleep, Gerda puzzled over the question. "Give them? Why, nothing. They helped me out of the goodness of their hearts."

"Don't be so stupid," said Ritva. "They were strangers, not kinfolk. Why would they help you, unless they wanted something from you?"

"In my country," said Gerda, "people do not steal from innocent travellers. They do not ambush them on the road and cut their throats. They do not kidnap them and hold them for ransom. Until I had the misfortune to meet you, I was treated with nothing but kindness and Christian charity. But I suppose, having a bandit for a father, you wouldn't know about that."

"He wasn't always a bandit," Ritva said. She spoke without rancour. "Not when he married my mother. He was a soldier then, in somebody or other's private army. The way he says it, he was drinking one night with soldiers from the garrison at Boden, and they were telling tales about the *birkarls* of old."

Gerda had read in history books about the *birkarls* — ruthless armed bands, licensed by the southern kingdoms, who robbed the reindeer herders in the guise of taxes.

"Well, my father thought this was a fine idea. But instead of robbing the reindeer folk of skins and the like, he thought he'd turn the tables by robbing southerners of their gold." She added, as an afterthought, "Mostly, though, he does it as an excuse to kill people."

"He killed the coachman, didn't he? And the coachman's boy."

"The coachman is dead," Ritva said. "As for the boy, I heard the men complaining that he ran into the woods. Probably the wolves got him."

Gerda rolled over, turning her back on Ritva so that the robber-girl would not feel the thudding of her heart. What if the wolves had not got the coachman's boy? What if he had made his way to Boden? What if the princess's nephew had called out his troops and even now was scouring the woods in search of her? She fell asleep at last, dreaming that she was home, in her own bed, between clean white sheets.

But as the nights lengthened, and the brief northern summer vanished in autumn wind and rain, and no one came, that small hope vanished.

Winter closed in. The wind howled through the pines; snow clogged the forest paths. The men of the camp settled down beside the roaring hearth for a winter-long night of drinking. Gerda's terror dulled into a numb despair, and finally into resignation. No one would come to rescue her now. She was trapped forever in this vast, filthy, Godforsaken place, where the wind shrieked like a wounded animal through broken walls, and wicked drunken brutes of men staggered and spat and cursed and fought, and she was at the mercy, always, of this harsh-tongued, ill-bred, spiteful girl who was her sole protector.

Now that day and night were the same, Gerda slept as long and as often as she could. It was her only means of escape. But even that respite was broken by feverish dreams. She dreamed of the gnawed bones of the coachman's boy, lying beside a forest path under rotting leaves and snow. She dreamed of her mother, watching thin and forlorn beside her window, weeping for a daughter who wrote no more letters, and would never return. And sometimes she dreamed of Kai, whose dark eyes stared at her from an ice mountain's blue-white depths, pleading desperately for release.

There was cold comfort to be had from Ritva. When Gerda woke in the dark, shivering and crying out, the robber-girl would mutter a curse and prod her with a sharp elbow, or rap her irritably on the side of the head. But sometimes it was Ritva herself who woke, whimpering and trembling like a frightened animal, in the black depths of the night.

CHAPTER FOURTEEN

The antlered man stepped out of the dark huddle of the pines. The lower half of his body was hidden in a swirl of ground-mist; his chest and shoulders were covered with a soft white pelt. Under the wide sweep of his horns, his face was wise and gentle. In her dream, Ritva spoke to him in the secret language of the animals. He smiled, and held out his hand to her. Just as their fingers touched, she woke.

And found that it was Gerda, snuggled beside her in their rabbit-skin nest, whose small damp hand gripped hers.

"You were talking in your sleep," Gerda said. She propped herself up on one elbow and stared down at Ritva. Her expression was half-curious, half-worried. "Was it in Finnish? I could not understand a word you said."

"Stupid one," said Ritva, yawning. "How should I know what language I speak in my sleep?"

"It must have been Finnish," said Gerda, with infuriating certainty.

"It was *not*," said Ritva. "I was talking to my guardian animal."

Gerda's eyes widened. "Oh," she said, caught off guard. "What sort of animal?"

"A white elk."

"I didn't know you had a guardian animal."

"There's a lot you don't know," said Ritva, unpleasantly.

"Do *I* have a guardian animal?"

"Everybody does. Even you. I think yours is a little white rabbit with pink eyes."

"You're making fun of me," said Gerda, offended.

"Of course I am. I like to make fun of you."

"I know," said Gerda, her eyes reproachful. "You tease every-body — me, your mother, Ba. You're a mean, cruel girl, and one day God will punish you."

Ritva gave a howl of laughter. "God! Which god?"

"Why, what do you mean? There is only one."

"Only one! Well, that can't be much use to anybody. My mother's people have dozens of gods. There are very little gods, and bigger gods, and great gods like Aijo, the father of shamans; and Baei've the Sun-God, and the God of Thunder, and the Old Man of the Winds."

"And where do you find all these gods?" Gerda's voice was scornful.

"Where? They are everywhere. They live in the forest, the river, the hearth fire, in the rocks and bushes — everything has a god in it."

I suppose she can't help it if she was raised a heathen, Gerda thought. Still, she wondered what their good Pastor Larssen would think of all this. Little gods who lived in rocks and trees, indeed! And how Kai would laugh! "Shall we go to church and pray to the benches and the altar-cloths?" she could imagine him saying. "Shall we sing a hymn to the door knocker?"

"If you had been brought up among Christian folk," said Gerda, "you would know there is only one God, and he lives in Heaven."

Ritva sat up in bed. She seized one of Gerda's plaits and yanked it so viciously that Gerda gave a shriek of pain. "Don't speak to me of the Christian god," Ritva hissed. "I know about him. He is the god of the southerners, who rounded up my mother's ancestors, and murdered their shamans and burned their drums. If you mention him to my mother, she will pull out her skinning knife and slit your throat."

Tears of pain and injured dignity oozed down Gerda's cheeks. She had long since lost her pocket handkerchief; these days she did as others did, and wiped her face on a filthy sleeve.

"That's not how it was," she said. "The missionaries were God-fearing men who built schools and churches to teach the gospel."

"And dragged the Saami people into those schools and churches by force, and made bonfires out of their drums," said Ritva. "One thing my mother taught me, is to hold my tongue when I don't know what I'm talking about." Gerda felt a rough hand grasping the wooden crucifix that still hung on its frayed ribbon at her throat. There was a sharp, angry tug, and the ribbon broke.

"This is what I think of your God," said Ritva. And beside her in the blackness, Gerda heard the brittle snap, snap of wood.

·When Ritva was asleep, Gerda fumbled in the dark for the broken pieces of her crucifix. Weeping with helpless rage, she hid them in the damp straw beneath her bed, where she prayed that Ritva would not find them. They were the only talismans left to her now, and the only reminders of her other life.

Chapter Fifteen

Water dripped from the eaves, and on the frozen river ice creaked and groaned. The birch trees budded and the days lengthened; the sun hung like a yellow flower in the midnight sky. On the first warm morning Ritva pulled the covers off Gerda's bed, seized her by both hands and dragged her to her feet.

"What's happening?" yawned Gerda, rubbing sleep out of her eyes.

"Winter's over, and both of us stink, and I'm going down to the river to wash. You're coming with me."

Gerda jerked her hands out of Ritva's grasp and crept back into her pile of skins.

Ritva stood over her, scowling. "What's the matter with you? Are you afraid of water?"

Gerda shook her head. "The men . . . the men will see us."

"Not today. They've all gone off hunting, and they won't be back till nightfall. Make haste, lazy one, the morning is half gone."

All Ritva had put on that morning was a long woollen shirt, gathered at the waist with a strip of leather. Bare-legged, she leaped and strutted down the slope to the riverbank, with Gerda trailing dolefully behind. The feel of the warm grass under her bare feet filled Ritva with excitement. At the river's edge she pulled her shirt over her head and tossed it to one side.

Naked, she gave a whoop of joy and leaped into the stream. The icy water cut like knives into her skin. "Come on," she shouted to Gerda, splashing water onto the bank.

Slowly Gerda peeled off her grimy layers of skirts and petticoats, until she stood shivering in the grey, bedraggled remnants of her shift.

Ritva stopped splashing. Covered with gooseflesh, she stood knee-deep in the frigid stream and stared at Gerda. How could she have failed to notice? Through the winter, all Gerda's childish plumpness had vanished. Her face, once round and flushed with health, was wan, her eyes dark-circled. Her limbs were white and thin as birch-saplings, her skin taut-stretched over flaring ribs and jutting hip-bones.

Ritva's belly tightened with dread. She knew all too well that when you lost flesh like that, sooner or later you died. She had seen it happen often enough with pigeons and rabbits. No matter how she coaxed them with crumbs or leaves they would turn their heads away, and before long she would find them lying cold and stiff in the straw.

Ritva clambered up onto the bank. "It's too cold," Gerda whispered through chattering teeth. Her arms were wrapped around her narrow chest.

"'You're cold because you've no fat on your bones." Fear sharpened Ritva's tongue. "Go on, put your clothes on. Why are you so skinny? We feed you, don't we?"

"I suppose." Gerda's lower lip trembled.

"Then why are you not eating?"

"How can I eat when I'm so miserable?"

"Miserable? You have a warm bed to sleep in. You have plenty of food to eat, and no work to do. Why should *you* be miserable?"

"Because," said Gerda, with weary patience, "I am not one of your pets, to be tied up with a rope and tormented for your amusement. I came here to find Kai. At night I dream that he is calling to me, pleading for my help. And you've kept me here, month after month, locked up like a rabbit in a cage."

"What do you mean, locked up?" Ritva was enraged by the injustice of this. "The door is open. If you hate it here so much, why don't you leave?"

Now it was Gerda's turn to be indignant. She snatched up a petticoat and yanked it angrily over her head. "Well, for one thing, you promised to cut my throat if I tried to run away."

"Yes, well," said Ritva. "Maybe I said that. I didn't think you'd believe me."

"The little one is sick," said Ritva's mother. She spoke with interest, but without much concern. "Her spirit has wandered halfway to the Land of the Dead."

"Do you think I cannot see for myself?" snapped Ritva. "Old woman, you must go and fetch it back."

"Huh!" said her mother, showing wide gaps in her bottom teeth. "You ask that of me, you who never speaks a word of kindness to me? Can't you see I am a tired old woman, who is hanging on to her soul by a thread? Such a journey would be the finish of me, for certain."

"Then I will go myself," said Ritva.

Shrewd black eyes peered out from their nests of wrinkles. "You? You think yourself a shaman, girl? You have much to suffer, before you can wear these robes, or ride this drum."

"The power is in me," Ritva said. "I have seen visions. My guardian animal has come to me in the night."

"Easy enough, to let your soul go free," said her mother. "But have you the power to call it back? I have seen others, who banged on a drum and thought they were ready for the journey. They are wandering yet, on the road to the Dead Lands, and their bodies have withered away to a bundle of hair and bones."

"I want to heal her," Ritva said.

"Then let her go. It's her heart that is sick, not her body. She pines like a wild thing kept on a chain."

"That's what *she* said," Ritva muttered.

"Then listen, for once. What use is she here, to anybody? Not even Henrik will want such a sad, skinny stick of a thing. Let her go now, before another winter sets in. Before she dies in this house, and her wandering spirit haunts our doorsill."

Ritva woke in some nameless hour of the night. Even the pigeons slept; there was no sound in the great hall but the faint snap of embers on the hearth. Her forehead felt sticky with sweat; her bones ached and it was hard to draw her breath. The thick stagnant air of the hall was like a blanket against her face. At last she got up, pulled on her boots and crept out into the luminous summer night.

She walked for a long time, wandering aimlessly along forest paths, filling her lungs with clean, pine-scented air, letting the night wind cool the fever that burned inside her. She felt dazed and disoriented, scarcely aware of her surroundings; she had no idea how far she might have strayed from the castle. Something was drawing her deeper and deeper into the trees, something that would not let her rest or turn back.

Near morning, she found herself in a small mossy clearing in a birch wood. The sun cast long blue shadows under the trees, where snow still lay in rotting patches. Never had she felt such bone-deep exhaustion. She sighed, and sat down on the damp ground, resting her head on her knees.

It could have been minutes, or days, that she huddled there. And then, as though her name had been spoken, she looked up.

The bear reared on his hind legs, an immense and terrifying shape, black as shadow against the silvery wall of birches. Ritva could smell the pungent wet odour of his pelt, feel his rank breath on her face. He lashed at her with one of his enormous paws. She felt his claws peel the flesh from her face and the scalp from her head, shred the clothes from her body. She shrieked in pain and terror as muscle and fat and tendons were ripped away. And then she stood shuddering in her naked bones. Her ribs clattered together; she looked down at her feet, saw the delicate framework of white twigs, the polished white knobs where her ankles joined her feet. She began to count all the bones in her body, giving each one a name — not in the Saami tongue, or in Finnish, or in any other human speech, but in the secret language of the animals. When she had finished, she felt no more pain, nor was she conscious of the whistling of the night wind between her ribs, the gnawing of the pre-dawn chill on naked vertebrae. She was flooded with calm, and lightness, and power; freed of everything that was transient, unessential; pared down to the hard imperishable bone.

And now she could hear all the voices of the forest calling to her.

"Hurry, hurry," howled the wind-spirit. "Would you spend another winter shut up in your father's house?" And the river-spirit joined in with her murmurous, insistent voice, "Go quickly, Ritva. This is the adventure you've dreamed of." The grasses, sly and insistent, whispered, "Life is short, Ritva.

Tomorrow will be too late."

Only the rock-spirits, stolid and earthbound, said "Stay, Ritva, stay. You must listen to us, for we are the oldest and wisest. What is this southern girl to you, that you would risk your life for her? She prays to the Christian god, who burned your drums and drove your mother's people into hiding. Let her go alone into the winter lands. Let her god save her from the wolf's jaws."

But the trees called out to her with all their voices joined, like a great chanting. "We are wiser than the rocks, for we are the children of the World-Tree. Our trunks join under earth with air; our branches hold the sky up. Go, Ritva. Travel our hidden paths. We will protect you."

The light had changed. Her throat was parched, her bladder ached, her belly churned with hunger; she guessed that she had slept the day away, and it was evening again.

When she reached her father's hall she found Gerda hovering anxiously in the forecourt.

"Thank goodness," Gerda said. "No one knew where you'd gone — I was sure the wolves had eaten you."

"Not wolves," said Ritva. She felt light-headed and weak, but unaccountably cheerful. "A bear."

Gerda's eyes widened, but before she could open her mouth to speak Ritva had seized her by the elbows and was dancing her madly through the gate and into the hall. "We'll rescue your Kai, little rabbit," panted Ritva, half out of breath. "I have made up my mind to it." The evening stew was simmering on the hearth. Ritva dipped out a ladle-full of broth, blew on it, and gulped it down. Then she began spearing chunks of meat and vegetables straight out of the kettle on the point of her knife. "Where's my mother?" she asked, with her mouth full.

"Gone gathering mushrooms," said one of the women.

"Ah," said Ritva. "She'll be out in the forest, then. All night, did she say?"

The woman shrugged. "Most like."

"Good," said Ritva, and as the women of the camp watched in horrified delight, she stepped over the invisible line that marked the boundary of her mother's *boasso*, her sacred space.

She lifted the shaman's robe from its hook, and settled it over her shoulders. It had a pungent, sweetish smell of medicinal herbs, and cured skins, and sweat. Then she picked up her mother's drum of bent wood and reindeer hide. Never before had she held it in her hands, or looked so closely at it. It was decorated with all kinds of signs and pictures — gods, humans, magic animals, hunting scenes, runic symbols — drawn in the red juice of alder bark. When her mother put a piece of wood on the tight-stretched drumskin, it danced about over these magic signs and foretold the future.

Ritva squatted in front of the drum. She drew a long breath, then picked up the reindeer horn prong and began the ritual that for so many years had disturbed her dreams. All through that night she chanted, and beat upon the drum. The world slipped away from her. Her flesh dissolved; her bones turned to air. She felt herself rising like smoke through the hole in the roof over the *boasso*. Above her was the Pole Star, that pinned in place the vast tent of the sky; below her, the shattered roof of her father's hall; and beyond, the winding ribbon of river and the dark sea of pines, spreading out to the world's rim. Her mind was flooded with a white fire that burned through darkness like the arctic sun. She thought of the far-seeing that her mother's people called *sjarat*, when the air was so clear that distances seemed to shrink, and the far seemed close at hand. But this was a gift of seeing infinitely stranger and more powerful than *sjarat*. Nothing was hidden from her gaze. She could see through solid earth and rock to the hidden world of the dead, where her mother had so often journeyed; but she knew that Gerda had no desire to travel in that grim land. Instead, she must chart her a path over forest and swamp and snowfield to the farthest, unknown edges of the world.

She was clinging to the back of a white elk, her guardian spirit, and the land moved like water beneath her. The air was alive with the crackling, whispering music of the stars. She flew through forests of larch and pine locked fast in the jaws of winter, a universe of trees unbroken by any path, where the eyes of wolves gleamed like yellow lanterns through the falling snow. She crossed vast swamps and treeless mossy wastes. She soared over fields of moon-white ice under a sky as black as a raven's wing. She saw glittering cliffs of ice rising out of an iron-dark sea. All across the sky the northern lights rippled and danced like a luminous curtain of silk. Snowflakes with the shapes of nameless animals devoured the breath upon her lips. Ice-daggers pierced her lungs. And at last, at the edge of the heavens, where earth and sky joined, she glimpsed the white windswept palace of the Woman of the North.

CHAPTER SIXTEEN

Gerda sat up, bleary-eyed and half-asleep, in the pre-dawn gloom. "What time is it?" she muttered crossly. For a moment or two, in the bewilderment of first waking, she thought she was at home in her own goosedown bed, under her clean white counterpane. But then she heard the cooing of the pigeons, smelled dung and woodsmoke, felt a rough hand shaking her by the shoulder. With a now-familiar clenching of her stomach, she remembered where she was.

"Get up," hissed Ritva. "Make haste. It's time to go. We must saddle Ba before my mother wakes."

Through all the months of her captivity Gerda had been desperate to resume her journey, regardless of its perils. Now, on the morning of departure, she felt her courage and her stubborn resolve wavering. Already the trees were turning red and gold; before long the first fierce squalls of autumn would sweep down over the hills. And yet it was the best time to travel. The roads were dry, the skies clear; the mosquitoes were gone, and the blackflies yet to come. These were the weeks when rich folk travelled north to their hunting lodges, and the pickings were good for Ritva's father and his men. This last week the camp had been empty but for the women and children, and a few boys and old men left to guard their chieftain's crumbling domain.

"Get up, little rabbit." Ritva tossed a much-mended woollen tunic into Gerda's lap. "Are you maybe changing your mind? Well, it's too late for that."

Gerda fumbled with the tunic lacings. "Ritva, are you sure you know the way?"

"We follow the Northern Lights, little rabbit — north to the edge of the Frozen Sea. My spirit flew on ahead to find the path, remember, and a long cold hungry journey it was."

While Ritva went to fetch Ba, Gerda groped in the straw under the bed until she found the pieces of her crucifix. Though they were beyond repair, the wood gone soft and spongy with damp-rot, she wrapped them carefully in a scrap of deerskin and put them away in her pack.

Old Ba gave them a sad, resigned glance when they laid a folded blanket and wooden pack-saddle over his bony spine, and laced on his saddle baskets. His muzzle was worn smooth with years of browsing for moss in the winter snows; his eyes had a tired, heavy, half-blind look.

Gerda watched as Ritva stuffed the saddle baskets full of warm clothes and stealthily gathered provisions — dried meat-strips, coffee, fur mittens, fur-trimmed caps, rain-capes to wear over their tunics when the weather turned wet and cold. As well, she strapped on two pairs of skis, woollen blankets to serve as bed-covers or tent-cloths, and two heavy, pungent wolf-skin coats. Finally, she bound the tent poles up into two bundles and attached them to either side of the saddle so that they trailed behind like the tail of a bird. Hanging from the saddle pommels were various bits of cooking equipment — a coffee grinder and kettle, a battered pot. With plenty of small game, and fish in the streams, they would not go hungry.

That first morning, as they crept out of the camp, they could feel the cold breath of approaching winter; but when the sun came up, the sky was a deep unbroken blue. The golden leaves of the birches shimmered in the slanting autumn light. Gerda's heart pounded; she felt dizzy and light-headed. She was like a caged bird, suddenly released into the wide, bright air.

At first the day's marches left Gerda bone-weary, aching in every joint, but now, as her appetite returned, so did her endurance. It was as though she were recovering from a long, exhausting illness. Striding along beside Ba and Ritva in her grass-lined Saami boots, she was filled with a nervous energy that lightened her steps and made her heart beat faster. She felt, now, that she could face whatever hardships lay ahead.

They spoke little as they travelled, but from time to time, in a burst of high spirits, Ritva would start to sing in a husky, tuneless voice. Most of her songs were rude soldiers' ditties that made Gerda blush and cover her ears; but sometimes, in a meditative mood, she sang snatches of old rune songs, or hummed and improvised her way through a Saami *joik*.

Thus Gerda learned of Stalo the Giant and his wife Lutakis the Treacherous; and of the Ulda who lived at the bottoms of lakes and rode on sleds drawn by white reindeer a-jingle with a thousand silver bells. Or sometimes the words were Ritva's own invention: "Who is the hero who will journey behind the Cave of the North Wind?" she would chant exuberantly, keeping time to her loping stride. "Who is the hero who will break the spell of the Terrible Enchantress?"

There were whortleberries and lingonberries in the bogs, and the bilberry bushes were heavy with fruit. In the pine forests, in the shade of rotting stumps, huge pale mushrooms sprang up like ghosts. They fished for perch and pike in the streams and ate them with bilberries stewed into a sauce, and they boiled strong, bitter coffee over their small fire.

Beyond the birchwoods and the pine forest lay high bare tundra, rolling endlessly before them like a moss-green meadow. One early evening they came to a lake set into a deep bowl of white-peaked mountains. The near side of the lake was lit by a faint blue glow, while the farther shore was washed in vivid rose-coloured light. A solitary turf-covered, dome-shaped dwelling, a *goattieh*, stood at the edge of the forest facing the lake. It looked like a small grassy hill with a thread of white smoke curling out of the top.

"We'd better let them know they have guests," said Ritva, as they drew near. She called loudly through the doorway of the *goattieh*, "Is anyone there?"

"Only me, and the mice," said a good-humoured voice.

They ducked in through the narrow entranceway, stepping around a stack of firewood. Every inch of the floor was carpeted with birch branches, except for the hearth in the centre of the room. There, an old woman sat surrounded by pots and pans and cauldrons. She was stirring something in a blackened kettle that hung on a long sooty chain suspended from a roof beam. Further along the beam were rows of dried cod and half-dried laundry. The smell in the *goattieh* was a rich mixture of smoke, boiled coffee, reindeer hides and fish.

Bright black eyes peered at them from a leathery, high-cheek-boned face. "Come in, come in," the woman said. "I've just made a fresh batch of cakes, in case anyone should happen by."

She poured strong salted coffee for them, and gave them flat bread baked on the hearthstones, and strips of smoked fish, and stewed reindeer meat. Everything, Gerda noticed, was full of reindeer hairs, but nonetheless tasted delicious after their long journey.

"You must stay with me tonight," the old woman said. "There is a shed behind the *goattieh* where you can tie up your beast." When they had devoured the last hearth-cake, the woman gave them reindeer hides to spread over the birch branches for their beds.

"Now then," she said, settling herself comfortably beside the hearth, "you must tell me what brings you to my humble door."

Gerda glanced at Ritva. Where to begin?

"I am helping my friend, because a woman has stolen her lover," said Ritva in a matter-of-fact voice, ignoring Gerda's indignant glare.

"Ah," said the old woman, grinning. "A romance. And who is this woman?"

"She is called the Baroness Aurore," said Gerda. There seemed little point, now, in contradicting Ritva's version of events.

"That's what she may call herself," said Ritva, "but my people know her by another name. My dead grandmother sang me a song about her. She is the Woman of the North, the Terrible Enchantress. She has taken Gerda's lover away to her kingdom at the northernmost edge of the world, and is holding him captive."

"And how do you happen to know this?" asked the old woman, pouring herself another cup of coffee.

"I sent my spirit on a journey, riding on the back of a white elk, and I saw him with my own eyes, in her ice palace at the world's rim, where the earth and sky meet."

"Ah," said the old woman, as if this was an entirely reasonable explanation. "Well, if you like I can tell you a story about this woman. It's only what I have heard, mind, and there are a great many stories in the world — you must decide for yourself which ones you want to believe. They say she was one of the wise ones who dwelt in the northern wastes, who lived in solitude with their books and manuscripts, and practised their wizard's arts. But you must be strong of spirit to deal with magic — otherwise, where you thought to be its master, instead you become its servant. She was a powerful wizard, but not powerful enough to control her magic, and in the end it possessed her. Now they call her the Drowner of Heroes and Devourer of Souls. Storm and fog and the icy cold of eternal darkness are her weapons. It was she who did battle with the magician Väinö when he tried to share her power. Once, they say, in a fit of spite she ripped the sun and the moon out of the sky and hid them away beneath a mountain."

Gerda, who had been listening in silence, thought of what Kai — cool, rational, level-headed Kai — would think of all this. "I don't believe in wizards, and sorceresses," she told the old woman. "They are tales to frighten children."

"Ah, well, little one," sighed the old woman. "Is it better, or worse, I wonder, to die at the hands of an enemy you don't believe in?"

"I only meant," said Gerda, confused, "that she is a woman, like any other — though cleverer, perhaps, and able to seduce people into doing what she wants. But I don't believe she has magic powers."

"Oh, don't you now?" murmured the old woman. "Well, I have no opinion, one way or another. I stoke my fire, and stir my soup, and tend to my own affairs. No doubt that is why I have lived as long as I have. But you're on the right road — I have heard that she likes to spend the early autumn at her lodge in Finnmark, before she returns to her winter palace."

"How much farther to Finnmark?" Gerda asked.

"Oh, you have a long way to go yet — a hundred miles or more — but if you hurry, maybe you can catch up with her.

There is a woman in Finnmark who can help you more than I — a woman of power. I will give you a letter of introduction. Have you a bit of paper about you?"

Ritva looked blank. Paper and pen were tools as exotic to her as spears and skinning knives were to Gerda. Out of habit, Gerda felt where her skirt pocket would have been, in an earlier existence. She shook her head.

"No? Never mind," said the old woman. She reached up and unhooked a dried codfish from the beam. "This will do in a pinch."

Face screwed with concentration, she used the point of a knife to scratch a series of runes on the back of the fish. "Mind you don't lose this, now," and she gave it to Ritva to put away in her pack.

Day by day they moved farther out of autumn into winter, trudging northward through a landscape of low hills covered with snow-clad pines, and over frozen marshes dotted with stunted fir. The days were grey and murky, the long nights glittering with starlight. Ba foraged under the powdery new snow for dried lichen and hidden summer greenery, digging down with his hooves and then thrusting his nose into the reindeer-moss beneath. They pitched their tent among tall rocks or clumps of trees — anywhere they could find shelter from the sudden snow-squalls that swept down without warning.

Then one day, in early dusk and driving snow, they came to a little *goattieh* huddled in the shelter of a cliff. There was no door, only a narrow window covered by a piece of hide, with firelight flickering behind. Ritva knocked boldly at the window, and after a moment someone pushed aside the hide and squinted out at them. "Come in, come in," a voice croaked. "Be quick, before all the heat gets out."

"I cannot leave my reindeer out here for the wolves to eat," said Ritva.

"You can keep one eye on him through the window," the voice said. Ritva tied Ba's reins to a stunted tree and clambered through the window, with Gerda following.

The voice belonged to the oldest, smallest woman Gerda had ever seen, a tiny wrinkled, wizened, toothless creature, all nose and chin and bushy white hair like a witch in a fairy tale. And yet there was nothing fearsome about her. Her eyes, as bright as river stones, were clever and kind.

"Why don't you have a door?" asked Ritva.

"Why would I want a door? My kinfolk bring me whatever I need to live, and hand it through the window. I never go out that way. If I ever leave, it's by the smoke-hole."

Gerda glanced up at the roof in puzzlement. It was true, the old woman was almost small enough to escape through the smoke-hole, but were those old bones agile enough for such a leap? Then, catching Ritva's eye, she understood: it was not the old woman's body but her spirit that came and went through that narrow hole.

The air in the room was stifling, choking. Gerda felt her whole body bathed in sweat under her heavy coat. The two of them began to peel off their winter garments, layer by layer, until they were down to tunics and trousers.

"Put your boots to dry on the hearthstones," the woman said.

"We've brought you a message," said Ritva. She looked a trifle foolish, holding out the stiff, smelly fish. But the old woman accepted it gravely, and read the runes with as much attention as if they were written on the finest deckled parchment.

"I see," said the old woman. She dropped the cod into the soup pot. "Well, my young ladies, I hope you have not bitten off more blubber than you can chew."

"I beg your pardon?" Gerda said.

"My friend the Saami woman tells me you have come seeking the Enchantress of the North. She and I are old enemies, and knowing her powers, I fear for the souls of two such innocents as yourselves."

"I know who you are," said Ritva, suddenly. "You are the woman who binds the winds. My mother spoke of you. She said you knew how to tie all the winds of the world together with a bit of twine, and when you choose to let all of them loose at once, forests topple, and the roots of the mountains creak."

"No offense to your mother," said the old woman, "but what a lot of nonsense people talk!"

"Can you teach me to bind the winds?" asked Ritva, pretending she had not heard.

"What for?" asked the woman slyly. "Are you planning a sea voyage?"

"No," said Ritva. "But if I am to rescue Gerda's friend from the Enchantress, I will need all the weapons I can find."

"But this is not your battle," the woman said. "It is Gerda's."

Ritva looked at her with startled disbelief. "What, that little one? My little rabbit? How will she fight the Terrible Enchantress? That is a task for heroes, for women of power."

"Like you? But Ritva, there is more than one kind of power. Never underestimate the power of innocence, of a good and trusting nature."

Ritva gave a shout of raucous laughter. "A trusting nature? Old woman, how long would I have survived if I had a trusting nature? The quickness of my wits, the knife in my hand, my two swift feet, that's what I trusted."

"Gerda trusted you. And you repaid her trust. As did everyone she met. How else has she come so far, survived so much, and remained unharmed? Unlike you, my girl — you will always have to fight for what you want. Maybe you will get it — but never without a struggle, never without cost."

"She survived because I saved her. My father would have slit her throat, or married her to some drunken lout who'd have beaten her black and blue."

"And why did you save her?" asked the old woman. "Was it only a whim, because you were bored with tormenting your mother and your poor old reindeer, and wanted a new pet?"

"Yes," Ritva started to say, and then faltered, staring at the old woman, whose level gaze, in return, seemed to see clear through Ritva's skull. "No," she admitted. "At first I thought I wanted her as a pet, someone to come running when I snapped my fingers . . . "

"But instead . . . ?"

Ritva grinned, half-sheepishly. "Instead, it was me who came running."

The old woman gave a small, satisfied sigh. "You see. You see what power she has. You will have your part to play, my girl. But if the boy's soul is to be set free, it is your little rabbit who must do it."

"But first we must find the Enchantress. They say she has a lodge at the edge of the Frozen Sea."

"Well, as to that, I fear you have arrived too late. You will need to make that sea-voyage after all. She has left her lodge in Finnmark and returned to her palace, which is somewhere north of Spitzbergen, beyond the Cave of the North Wind, in the midst of the Frozen Sea."

Gerda's heart felt like a lump of ice in her chest. To have come so far, to have suffered so much, and then to be told that the worst part of the journey still lay before them . . .

"Where did you learn this, old woman?" Ritva asked.

The woman looked sharply round at her. "And where did you learn your manners, my girl? Maybe the wind told me, whistling through the smoke-hole. Isn't it enough that I have told you what you wanted to know?"

Ritva stared down at her boots, abashed.

"Just over there, behind my house, is a stream flowing north. Follow its banks until it joins a river. Follow the river north — it will lead you to a fjord where cod fishermen come to mend their nets. And (this with a mocking glance at Ritva) "if you want to know where I learned this, I made the trip with my kinfolk many a springtime, when they took the reindeer to graze on the high tundra above the sea."

"And then?"

"Follow the cliff path down to the shore. If you are lucky you may find a boat to hire. But you must go quickly, before winter comes to the Frozen Sea and the pack ice closes in."

"Gerda, help me put up the tent," said Ritva. "We'll sleep beside Ba, and leave at first light."

"Wait," said the old woman as they were preparing to set out in the morning. She reached through the window and thrust something into Ritva's hand. It was a small reindeer-skin pouch, with a drawstring of twine. "No, no, you must not open it yet," she shrilled, as Ritva, curious as always, tried to loosen the three knots that held it closed.

"When?" asked Ritva. She held up the pouch and peered at it. To all appearances it was empty.

"You will know when the time comes," said the old Finnmark woman.

"Now go with the wind, for time is wasting."

Chapter Seventeen

They pushed north along the riverbank beyond the last straggle of stunted birch, crossing bleak stretches of tundra where nothing grew but grey, prickly reindeer moss.

Thus they came at last to the edge of the land, where a windswept bluff overlooked an endless, heaving waste of iron-grey water. Below them was a desolate shoreline, half-glimpsed through fog — but neither village, nor fishboats, nor any sign of human habitation were to be seen.

Gerda stared down through the mist in stricken silence. This was what her wilful stubbornness had led them to. They could go no further; must they turn, now, and retrace their steps across those empty miles of marsh and forest, with the northern winter settling in?

"The old woman was mistaken," she said at last. "No one comes here. There are no fishermen. There are no boats." Her throat ached with shame and self-pity. "I was wrong to bring you here. It's all my fault."

Ritva's reply was lost in a sudden gust of wind. Gerda leaned closer. "You were not wrong," Ritva said, her hands cupped around her mouth. "In my dream-journey, on the back of the white elk, I flew over this place. I saw boats, and fishermen. The old woman spoke the truth."

A steep, stony path led down the side of the bluff into a rocky cove, sheltered by the fjord's high flanking cliffs. The fog grew thicker as they descended, swirling and billowing around them. Underfoot was a treacherous floor of smooth round stones, slick with damp and seaweed.

"Maybe around that point . . . " said Ritva, not very hopefully. She picked her way gingerly across the rocks and disappeared beyond a promontory jutting almost to the water's edge. "Come and look, come and look!" Gerda heard her shouting after a moment. Her voice was shrill with excitement.

Around the point was another, larger cove; and just offshore, pitching and swaying on the surge of the incoming tide, lay a sloop with furled sails. She was flying the blue Norwegian cross.

Ritva danced up and down on the rocks. "I told you there'd be a boat!" she shrieked.

"Not a boat, Ritva, a ship! A proper sailing ship." Gerda could just make out the letters on the hull: the *Cecilie*.

On a narrow strip of sand out of reach of the tide a dinghy was beached. Beside it crouched a blonde-bearded man who appeared to be mending a sail.

Gerda clambered onto a tumble of weed-slimed rocks and waved her arms. "Hallo," she shouted in Danish, over the clamour of wind and waves. "Hallo! Can you hear me?"

The man glanced up from his work. At the sight of Gerda, his mouth fell open with such a comical look of surprise that she began to giggle — helplessly, foolishly, out of sheer relief.

The man got to his feet and strolled toward the two girls. He was a big, burly man, with a leathery wind-tanned face. He looked up at Gerda and Ritva with quizzical blue eyes, and said, in good Danish, "How can I help you, my young friends? If it's the rest of your herd you're looking for, I haven't seen them."

At that instant Gerda saw herself, and Ritva, through the sailor's eyes — two half-grown boys dressed from head to foot in skins and furs, feet big and shapeless in grass-stuffed boots, nothing showing under their caps but chapped lips, wind-burned cheeks, a few greasy locks of cropped-off hair.

Gerda hesitated, waiting for Ritva to reply; but Ritva, oddly, was hanging back, looking uncertain and ill at ease.

Gerda drew herself up as tall as she could, met the sailor's bright blue gaze, and said, with all the boldness she could summon, "We're not looking for our reindeer, we're looking for work. Do you have work to give us?"

The man laughed. "Well, we've not much need for cabin-boys, unless the cook could use a hand. From the sounds of it you're Danish-born, like me — and we're both of us a long haul from Copenhagen. Further still, before this voyage is over — we're bound for Spitzbergen Island."

"As are we," said Gerda.

"Not for the walrus hunt, I'll be bound."

Gerda shook her head. The best lie, she thought, is the one that lies closest, in most particulars, to the truth.

"I must go to Spitzbergen in search of my elder brother," she said. "My mother is a widow, and we are her only two sons."

"And what is your brother doing on Spitzbergen? There is nothing there but rock and ice — and walruses."

"And lichen," said Gerda. "It seems there is also quite a large quantity of that. My brother is a student of botany, and he has gone to Spitzbergen to classify the various sorts of lichen according to Dr. Linnaeus's rules of taxonomy."

"I hadn't heard about that," said the sailor.

"No, I dare say you wouldn't," said Gerda gravely. "The expedition was privately funded, and the sponsor wished to avoid publicity."

"Yes, I see," said the sailor, who quite obviously did not.

"For fear of attracting the attention of rival botanists," elaborated Gerda, warming to her subject. "But something has gone amiss, we have had no word for months, and we fear that the expedition has come to disaster. My poor mother has been distraught. She can neither eat nor rest. And so I have travelled all the way from Copenhagen in search of my brother." She paused for effect. "Or his unfortunate remains."

"It looks like you're in luck," said the blonde sailor. "The Captain says we can spare a couple of hammocks in the fo'c'sle, and you can earn your passage by fetching and carrying for the cook."

"And our reindeer?"

The sailor gave a snort of laughter. "What, that old bag of bones? Turn him loose and let him forage."

Gerda was glad that Ritva understood so little Danish. "He's too old and too tame to fend for himself," she said. "We can't leave him behind."

"Well, we'll see what the Captain says about that," said the sailor.

The Captain, who luckily had a sense of humour, let them tie Ba up in the *Cecilie's* cargo hold. "Better hope we don't run into pack ice," he told Gerda. "If we get trapped, he'll go in the stewpot."

"I understand," said Gerda unhappily. Ritva blew in Ba's ear and tweaked his nose to show her affection; then they left the old beast with a handful of reindeer moss, and settled themselves on deck among the crates and barrels. For Gerda there was a comforting familiarity in the seacoast smells of tar and hemp and brine.

"What's a walrus?" Ritva wanted to know. "Can you eat it?"

"I dare say," replied Gerda, "if you were hungry enough. But I think they are hunting them for their ivory. I've seen a picture of one — it's a huge creature, big as an ox, with two great long tusks like an elephant's, and it lives in the sea."

"Elephant?" said Ritva blankly.

"Oh dear," sighed Gerda. She launched into a description of an elephant, from illustrations she remembered studying in her natural history books.

"Don't be so stupid," said Ritva. "You know there's no such beast. There's no such thing as a walrus, either." She leaned back against a barrel of salt beef, closed her eyes, and went to sleep.

Of the first day of the voyage, they remembered little. A stiff wind came up and set the vessel to pitching and heaving.

Too wretched with seasickness to move or talk, they lay in their hammocks in the dark airless fo'c'sle, half-choked by the reek of their own garments and the pungent stench of whale-oil lamps.

When they woke next day the wild tossing of the ship had subsided. They climbed out onto the deck into a fierce blaze of sunshine. The sea was calm, and green as meadow grass, a shimmering light-drenched expanse upon which a few huge ice floes floated gracefully as lily pads. In the distance they could see icebergs looming like mountains of blue-white glass.

"So you've found your sea legs, have you?" said the first mate. "Get below, the pair of you — the cook wants to know where you've been hiding."

domestic

In the galley, the cook kept them busy stoking the fire, scrubbing pots, stirring porridge, chopping vegetables for the stew.

"Might as well have stayed home," grumbled Ritva, peering queasily into a kettle of salt cod. Her face still had a faintly greenish look.

As they sailed northwest towards the coast of Spitzbergen, the sky darkened again, and the wind rose. Soon the surface of the sea was littered with thousands of ice floes, like huge white platters that collided and crunched together with a ceaseless noise of scraping and grinding, piling one on top of the other and up-ending and congealing into walls and towers and parapets. By next morning they were surrounded by a pitching, growling, churning immensity of ice.

As the wind grew stronger, the current battered their ship against the whirling floes. The *Cecilie* feinted and tacked, scurrying after corridors of open water, which narrowed and closed as they approached. Meanwhile the air grew misty, and the cold drizzle that had been falling throughout the day turned suddenly to snow.

All night Gerda lay awake in her hammock, listening fearfully to the grinding and grating and thudding of the ice. Now and then the ship's timbers groaned, and the vessel shuddered like a wet dog. Before dawn the noise had grown to a steady thunder. Feet pounded into the fo'c'sle. Lanterns bobbed and weaved in the dark as the watch roused the rest of the crew.

Gerda rolled to the fo'c'sle deck and fumbled for her boots and coat. Ritva was still asleep, cocooned in her hammock with her blanket pulled over her head. Gerda shook her by the shoulder till she stirred, groaned, and sat up.

"What do you want?" snarled the robber-maid, clawing her hair out of her eyes.

"Get up — we all have to get up. I think we're abandoning ship."

Someone held up a lantern close to Gerda's face. She blinked in its sudden glare. "Here, get moving, you two — get out on deck." All around her Gerda could hear orders being shouted, things being shifted, the scrape of heavy objects across the boards.

Gerda and Ritva paused for a moment at the top of the ladder to ease their aching shoulder muscles and catch their breath. The wind had died, but the air was bitter cold, searing its way into their lungs. Everywhere on the foredeck stood bundles of fur garments, bedrolls, oil lamps, cartons of canned goods, muskets and harpoons. All the galley equipment — pots, pans, kettles — had been stacked nearby. The crew were dragging the last boxes of equipment and sacks of provisions from below decks. Gerda looked up, saw that the sails and rigging were coated in frost. The sun was a faint pink stain on the horizon.

And then she saw the ice — a greyish-green jumble of walls and slabs and ridges, rising level with the rails and stretching as far as the eye could see. Amidships snow was piling up above the rails, and as she watched, the whole loose powdery mass toppled over onto the deck. She clung to Ritva in terror as their ship was ground and squeezed and twisted, and her shrieking timbers torn apart. The *Cecilie's* bow shot up in the air, her stem was wrenched sideways as though caught in a gigantic vise.

"Get to work," someone shouted at them, and startled out of their panic, they took hold of a sack between them and dragged it over the rails, onto the ice.

Just then the ship gave a kind of groan and listed further onto her side. Abruptly Ritva let go of the sack, and without a word turned and raced back to the ship.

Long anxious moments passed. At every creak of the timbers Gerda's stomach twisted itself into a tighter knot. Another minute, she thought . . . one minute more and I will go after her.

And then Ritva reappeared, leading the old reindeer over the tilted railing onto the ice. He was trembling, and his eyes rolled wildly in their sockets, but he seemed unhurt.

"Oh, praise Heaven," cried Gerda, running to meet them. Without stopping to think, she threw both arms around Ritva. "I was so afraid you'd got trapped." She felt Ritva stiffen, heard her hiss a warning, and remembering that she was no longer Gerda Jensen, but a cook's boy, she dropped her arms and hastily stepped back.

"We nearly didn't get out," said Ritva. Her tone was matter-of-fact. "One side of the hold is caved in, and it's a wonder this poor old brute wasn't crushed as flat as a hearth-cake."

She tickled Ba absent-mindedly behind his ears to calm him. Snorting, he rubbed his nose against her cheek.

By afternoon the ship was all but stripped of supplies. Everything, including three large sledges and two of the boats, had been carried out onto the ice, and canvas tents were thrown up.

Gerda was too exhausted to spare much thought for tomorrow. She ate the bread and butter and chocolate that was passed around, drank the whey milk the cook had warmed over a blubber lamp.

How could she have imagined the Captain was joking when he talked of being trapped in pack ice? Then a dreadful thought occurred to her. That was not the only joke the Captain had made. She sought out the first mate, who was driving tent pegs into the ice.

"You must not kill Ba. He is a good and faithful beast, and will serve us well if we must walk across the ice to Spitzbergen."

The first mate looked round in a puzzled way. Then he grinned. "What, that old reindeer? No, lad, we are well provisioned, he won't go in the pot yet awhile. And I doubt we'll be walking as far as Spitzbergen."

That night Gerda and Ritva stood with all hands in the shadow of their crushed ship, listening to the captain speak. A cold silvery mist was rising around them; the wind, keen as a knife, riffled the men's beards and tugged at the corners of the tents. Their breath smoked.

"It's not as bad as it seems," said the captain, though his tired, strained face belied those encouraging words. Perhaps, thought Gerda, he hopes with calming speeches to ward off the panic that seizes men who are trapped in the arctic wastes. She had read about that paralyzing fear in explorers' tales; she had never thought to experience it herself.

"Mr. Stemo's been aloft with his spyglass," the captain was saying. "He's spotted what looks like an island, no more than twenty miles off. We've plenty of provisions — and when those run out, they say the flesh of arctic foxes is good as venison, and a polar bear or two will keep us alive for months. Plenty of icebound sailors before us have survived the winter cozily enough."

"Aye, and plenty starved, and froze as stiff as kipfish where they lay," Gerda heard one sailor mutter; but he kept his voice low, so only those standing nearest him heard, and gave him nervous grins.

Next morning they set out across the pack ice in search of land. With canvas bands strapped across their chests, the men took turns hauling the two salvaged cutters and three heavily-laden sledges. It was slow, hard, treacherous going, dragging those cumbersome loads hour after hour over the ridged and buckled icescape. The boats were weighed down with tents, cookstoves, kettles, stewpots, fur-lined deerskin sleeping bags, spare boots and moccasins, caps and mittens, tobacco, ammunition. On the sledges were barrels of salt meat and hardtack; casks of flour and oil, and dried cloudberries to ward off scurvy; hogsheads of wine and beer.

They sank to their knees in mush-ice, edged their way around hummocks, nervously skirted cracks and fissures with black water showing through. Ritva trudged silently beside Gerda, sullen-faced but uncomplaining. Ba's load was lighter now; their own gear had been lost with the ship.

When darkness overtook them the sailors threw up tents on the ice, and they crawled into their clammy bedrolls. Gerda slept little that night. All around her she could hear the ice creaking and groaning. She thought of children in her own village who had ventured onto the frozen Sound at break-up time, and had been swept out to sea. How fragile it was, how impermanent, this brittle crust of ice on which she lay. How long before it began to splinter, shatter, letting the bottomless black waters break free?

But in the morning, waking to a glittering white world under a cloudless sky, her spirits lifted, and that afternoon they reached solid ground.

They dragged the sledges onto a grey beach littered with huge boulders brought down from the icefields. Scattered up the treeless slopes were brilliantly coloured, lichen-encrusted rocks, and bright clumps of saxifrage blooming amid patches of snow.

"Is this Spitzbergen Island?" Gerda asked one of the sailors, with faint hope. He shook his head. "Some Godforsaken rock in the middle of the ice, not big enough to be on the charts."

The crew hoisted the Norwegian flag, and then they gathered around a driftwood fire to eat their evening meal of pemmican stew. "It looks like we'll be spending the winter here," grumbled the seaman sitting next to Gerda. "I thought all along we were pushing our luck, so late in the season. It looks snug enough now, but wait until midwinter, when rations run short, and hoarfrost grows on our faces while we sleep."

"Well, it was walruses we came for, and walruses we've got," said the first mate dryly, as they listened to the roaring and snorting of the great sea-beasts.

In the morning Gerda and Ritva made themselves useful by collecting driftwood and dry birds' nests for fuel, while the men went out with muskets to lay in a store of meat and skins for winter. Then the crew set to work to build a driftwood hut, sinking the floor three feet into the ground, and chinking the cracks in the walls with gravel and moss. For the roof they used walrus skins stretched over a driftwood rooftree and held in place with stones suspended from rawhide thongs. To enter the hut they crawled on hands and knees through a tunnel and then pushed their way past heavy bearskin curtains. Inside there were plank beds covered with bearskins, and blubber lamps that shed a smoky light.

"You know we can't stay here," said Ritva.

"I know," Gerda mumbled into her pillow. She was warm at last, her belly was full; she could think of nothing but sleep.

"We must find Kai . . . but Ritva, first let me rest a little."

"Rest all you like — your precious Kai has waited this long, he can wait a little longer. But I meant, we can't spend the winter here. How long do you think it will be before they discover we are women, not boys?"

Gerda rolled over and gazed blearily up at Ritva. "And what if they do?"

Ritva snorted. She parroted Gerda's words in a high, mincing voice. "'And what if they do?' Can you still be so innocent, after spending a winter in my father's hall?"

"Oh, surely not," said Gerda, shaken. "These are not bandits; these are honourable men. They would never molest a Danish citizen."

"You think not?" said Ritva. "They are men, like all other men, and we'll be shut up in the dark with them from now till spring. I keep my knife in my sleeve, and you'd better do the same."

Now Gerda was wide awake. "And when they run out of food, they will eat Ba."

"That too," said Ritva grimly. "We must go soon, before the Long Night sets in."

"But how shall we travel?"

"As before. On foot. Northward, across the ice. We must find the Cave of the North Wind. Beyond that lies the Snow Queen's Palace.

Chapter Eighteen

For weeks Gerda and Ritva had been gathering lichen and dried herbage for fodder, and grass to line their boots. They lamented the loss of their skis and tent, their fishing gear and pots and kettles, abandoned in the *Cecilie's* hold, but Ritva was a determined scavenger and an accomplished thief. There were candles and tins of chocolate stuffed under her pillow, and stolen friction matches in her pocket, wrapped up in a scrap of sealskin to keep them dry. Hidden away in an ice-chest among the rocks were strips of seal and walrus meat pilfered bit by bit from the cook's stores.

"We won't starve," said Ritva with satisfaction, as she added another handful of ship's biscuits to the cache behind her bed. "Now hope that the sky stays clear, so we can find our way by the Pole Star . . . "

"And by this too," said Gerda. She reached under her blankets.

"What's that?" Curious, Ritva prodded the object in Gerda's hand.

"A compass," said Gerda, with a trace of smugness. "I saw it in one of the smashed boats, and it seemed a pity to leave it behind."

"What's it for?"

Gerda looked at her in astonishment. "You mean you've never seen a compass?" She held it up in the murky lamplight.

110

"Watch the needle. It points the way straight to the North Pole. When you have a compass, you don't need to see the stars."

The night sky glittered like a gigantic chandelier as they crept out of the hut and loaded their hoarded provisions into Ba's saddle-baskets. Fresh snow lay thick underfoot, and ice-glazed drifts were packed to the top of the shelter. Ba pushed his nose into Ritva's palm, and stamped his hooves as though impatient to be off. Swaddled in sweaters and reindeer tunic and fur-lined wolfskin coat, Gerda felt almost too cumbersome to walk, but she could feel the sharp sting of the icy wind on her face, and when she took off her mitts to tighten Ba's laces, her fingers turned blue and numb.

The quivering compass needle pointed their way north.

Everything known, familiar, had been left behind in the walrus-hunters' hut. The only sounds, now, were the shrilling of the wind and the crunch of snow under their boots, and from time to time the ominous rumble and screech of shifting ice. Sometimes they felt shockwaves running beneath their feet, as though somewhere in the distance immense slabs of ice were toppling.

The moon came out and flooded the broken snowscape with its chill white light. Never had Gerda imagined a scene so beautiful, or so forbidding. There was something dreamlike, hallucinatory, about this northward journey. Always before there had been lakes and rivers, hills and forests to help them chart their way. Now there were no more landmarks, and the thin shell of ice upon which they walked was like a vast unfinished puzzle, the pieces endlessly lifted and turned and shuffled by a giant hand.

Gerda had not thought it was possible to be so lonely. Though she was grateful for Ritva's steadfast presence, each of them, trudging silently through that frozen world, was locked in her own solitude. Is there anything more frightening, Gerda mused, than to be utterly alone with one's own thoughts? It was no wonder that arctic travellers panicked and went mad.

I will not think, she promised herself. I will not think of anything at all. If she let herself dwell for so much as an instant on the journey ahead, she knew she would fall to her knees on the ice and weep with helpless terror.

When they were too exhausted to go on, they threw up a makeshift shelter with poles and blankets, wrapped themselves in reindeer hides, and took turns to sleep. With daylight, Gerda saw that they had been lying on a narrow island of solid ice surrounded by a crazy-quilt of thin cracks. Here and there she could see gaping fissures with black water showing through. She roused Ritva; they fed Ba, breakfasted on some frozen strips of walrus meat, drank some melted snow, and plodded onward.

That second day dawned clear and windless. Through the brief hours of sunlight they trudged over ice-rubble and plains of soft loose snow. The sky changed from a bright wintry blue to turquoise, and then to ultramarine. On the southern horizon a pale red sliver of sun vanished in mauve-coloured haze. Soon the last of its light faded.

"Oh, look," said Gerda, awestruck, as the black sky filled with swirling ribbons and darting, flickering shafts of rainbow colour. "Ritva, look, the northern lights!"

"I see them," said Ritva impatiently. She added, with sour irony, "Why are you whispering? Who's going to hear you?"

And Gerda realized that her voice was as hushed as if she were in church.

Somewhere in the near distance there was a thunderous crash; the ice shuddered and rocked beneath their feet. Ritva caught hold of Ba's collar as he reared in panic. In the shimmering light of the aurora they saw a huge crack opening up not twenty paces ahead.

An ice-block the size of a cottage thrust halfway out of the fissure, and then slipped back. There was a grinding, splintering sound, and with a jolt the ice tilted sharply beneath them. Suddenly everything seemed to be moving, shifting, eddying. It was as though some huge sea-creature was threshing wildly beneath the ice.

Gerda's heart gave a sick lurch as she watched a black, wind-broken expanse of water widening before them. Ever since they had abandoned the *Cecilie* this was the thing she had dreaded most, the fear that had haunted her restless sleep. They were adrift, at the mercy of wind and tide, on an ice floe hardly bigger than the Princess's swansdown bed.

Gerda tugged off one of her mittens and groped for the compass. They seemed to be moving in an erratic but more or less northerly direction. "God is looking after us," she told herself sternly. If she clung to that thought, perhaps she could slow the frantic thudding of her heart. Aloud, she said, "We're drifting towards the Pole, Ritva. You'll see, it will be all right, maybe the sea will carry us all the way to the Snow Queen's palace."

There was no answer. She turned to look at Ritva. Frost glittered on the woollen scarf that half-covered the robber-maid's face. Above it, her eyes were wide and terrified. She was leaning against Ba, her hip pressed into his bony flank.

She is more frightened than I, thought Gerda, with a sudden shock of realization. *She is more afraid of the sea than I was afraid of the wilderness, or the robber's camp.*

A fierce gust from the northeast sent their ice-raft spinning. They were moving faster now. Gerda stared at the compass needle in dismay. They were travelling steadily southwest, losing whatever distance they had gained.

Gerda sent up a silent, panic-stricken prayer. "Please, God, let the wind shift again. Please, God — send us a wind from the south."

And then she remembered: a doorless hut, the smell of smoke and dried fish and reindeer stew, and an old woman putting something into Ritva's hand. What had she whispered to them, that old woman who kept the winds of the world bound up in a sack? *When the time comes, you will know.*

"Ritva, where is the bag the Finnmark woman gave you?"

"What?" Ritva clung to Ba's collar, as a shipwrecked sailor clings to a sinking mast.

"The skin bag. Do you have it still?"

Ritva nodded. Still clutching Ba with her other hand, she dug awkwardly under her coat and the tunic beneath.

Gerda seized the pouch, and with numb fingers picked clumsily at the first of the knots.

Sudddenly the pouch began to swell like a blown-up bladder, the skin growing parchment-thin as it stretched to twice, thrice, ten times its size. "Help me," Gerda shouted, tightening her grasp on the strings. The bag, still swelling, swayed and tossed above her like a giant hot-air balloon. Feet planted apart, backs braced, they struggled to hold the bag against the insistent tug of the wind. Then, just as it was about to lift them both off their feet, there was a shrill hiss, like steam escaping, and some immense, invisible thing shrieked its way out.

In the open channel before them, water churned and swirled as though stirred by a gigantic spoon; columns of water spun upward, glittering with starlight. And then suddenly the wind seized them, spun them round, propelled them into another widening channel, where the current caught them in its teeth and swept them northward.

All the rest of that night they drifted towards the Pole Star. It was so bitter cold, now, that hoarfrost grew on everything — on Ba's hooves and antlers, on the saddle-packs, on the shoulders of their wolfskin coats. Their eyelashes froze; their lungs ached.

No sun rose that morning; before dawn an icy fog, thick as oat-porridge, had settled around them.

Then, towards afternoon, the mist thinned, and straight in their path, towering hundreds of meters against the steel-grey sky, they saw a mountain of black, ice-fissured rock.

At that moment their ice-floe began to spin wildly, like a leaf caught in a whirlpool. Ritva and Gerda clung to each other, and to Ba, as wind and water tossed and whirled them faster and faster towards the black mountain's base. But just as it seemed they would be dashed to bits against the rocks, a narrow opening, a cavern mouth, rushed up to meet them, and the sea, capricious as ever, sucked them straight into the mountain's heart.

Abruptly, the wild motion stopped, and they found themselves floating in a huge, vaulted space filled with a ghostly bluish light. On either side rose black, frost-streaked walls of granite. Pillars of ice stood in ranks, like watchful giants; long, glinting clusters of icicles dripped from the roof. Far ahead they could see a faint grey glimmer, a way out.

And then, waking somewhere in the dim grottos along the cavern walls, came the north wind's voice. It began as no more than an indrawn breath, a sigh, a gentle whisper of air in that echoing silence. But swiftly, surely, it gathered strength. Its sound, now, was the shrilling of the storm through snowbound passes, the creaking of masts in a black squall, the blizzard rattling in frozen shrouds. It was the cry of a wolf, a curlew's scream. It was the beating of enormous icy wings. The wind tore the words from their lips, the breath from their lungs. It battered their fragile raft of ice against the glistening cavern walls.

Then, as suddenly as they had entered, they were through, like a cork exploding from a bottle.

On the other side of the mountain, beyond a narrow channel of dark water, lay a world of utter emptiness and silence, a world of profound night. The moon hung like a great pewter dish in a cobalt sky. Trackless snowfields, stained with violet shadows, stretched away to the dark line of the horizon, where they vanished into a silvery mist.

For a long moment neither could find breath to speak. Finally, in a tired whisper, clutching the robber-maid's mittened hand for comfort, Gerda said, "We've done it, Ritva. We've passed through the Cave of the North Wind. We've come to the Snow Queen's country, where earth and day end."

And yet, strangely, she felt nothing — neither relief, nor joy at their survival. Sick with cold and exhaustion, she was aware only of an awful hollowness in her stomach, a sinking dismay at what still lay ahead.

Chapter Nineteen

No winds blew, in this dark and silent country behind the north wind's cave. The only sounds were the faint snuffling of Ba's breath and the crunch of his hooves through the falling snow. To Gerda's blurred, exhausted vision, those huge flakes seemed to grow larger and larger, taking on fantastic shapes, like knotted serpents, or many-headed beasts.

They pushed on through loose powdery drifts, sinking up to their knees. And softly, silently, relentlessly, the snow fell. They had come to a place outside of time, beyond geography: where snowfields flowed on and on under the frozen stars to the world's rim, where earth and heaven meet.

"I can go no farther," said Gerda in a faint, pleading voice. She was past weariness, at the edge of collapse. "Please, Ritva, let me rest for a little." She had lost all feeling in her hands and feet. Her chest ached; she could feel the muscles of her legs quivering with fatigue. She had forgotten what it was like to sleep.

"Don't be a fool, if you stop, you'll freeze," Ritva snapped at her. "A few more miles — "

"Or a hundred, or a thousand?" asked Gerda, in despair.

"No. Remember, I made this journey once before, in my vision."

And then the snow stopped, and the sky cleared. They could see the stars now, an infinite number of glittering pinpoints in

117

a high dark canopy. And all at once the sky was ablaze with
arrows and archways and rippling curtains of flame. In the
northern distance, across the shadowy snowfields, stood towers
and turrets and parapets of crystal, glimmering rose-pink and
gold and apple-green.

Snowdrifts clung to the window ledges of the Snow Queen's
palace. The tall arched panes glittered with a wintry, ice-blue
light. The great doors of crystal and silver stood ajar, unguarded;
a powdering of snow filmed the milk-white marble tiles of the
courtyard within.

No hearthfires burned in those vast, chill rooms — only
the cold and eerie flames of the aurora borealis, blazing down
through crystal skylights, flickering across the icy floors. They
could hear the faint glassy tinkle of chandeliers, the whistling
of the wind down endless, empty halls. There was a kind of
music, too — high, keening, crystalline notes infinitely, pierc-
ingly sustained, like tones struck on a goblet's rim. The sound
was like a knifeblade in the base of Gerda's skull. She clapped
her hands over her ears to shut it out.

Nothing had prepared Gerda for a palace so magnificent —
and so utterly devoid of warmth and comfort. *No one human
could live in this place*, she thought. And she shuddered at a
sudden chilling intimation: living here, what might Kai have
become?

Tears of weakness, exhaustion, desolation, leaked from her
eyes, and froze into beads of crystal on her cheeks. The cold
had crept into her muscles and bones, had wrapped itself round
her heart.

From wall to wall, in the Great Hall of the Snow Queen's palace, spread a lake of ice. The surface was fractured into thousands of interlocking pieces, like a gigantic Chinese puzzle. In the middle of the hall stood a tall, spare figure in a white ermineskin coat.

Gerda's heart began to race; suddenly she felt dizzy and faint. She clutched Ritva's arm, half-leaning against her for support. "It's him," she whispered through numb, chapped lips. "It's Kai." And then, in bewilderment: "Ritva, whatever can he be doing?"

She moved closer, stepping cautiously over the broken surface. As she watched, Kai sank to his heels, crouching awkwardly on the ice, and with both hands prised up a flat, heavy, puzzle-shaped piece. Straightening with the slow, painful effort of an old man, he dragged the ice fragment for a few meters, hesitated, and laid it down again. Then he stood, head bent, seemingly lost in thought.

"Kai," Gerda shouted out to him. "Kai! It's me, it's Gerda!" Her words bounced back to her, tauntingly, from the frost-rimed ceiling, the glassy white walls. The air crackled with cold. Kai's head lifted for an instant, turned slightly towards her. She drew in her breath to shout again. The cold pierced her lungs. But Kai had looked away, was staring down at the ice at his feet.

"Go to him, fool," hissed Ritva. She put her hands on Gerda's shoulders, gave her a determined shove.

The broken ice crunched under Gerda's feet. Her breath, freezing in front of her face, whispered like torn tissue paper.

"Kai — don't you know me? Won't you look at me?" She could hardly speak for the huge, aching lump in her throat.

The bent figure lifted its head. Red-rimmed, dark-shadowed, Kai's eyes seemed to stare straight through her. Gerda clasped his gloveless hands in her own. They were bloodless, brittle as frozen twigs, blue-white with cold.

He was like a figure carved from ice: blind, deaf, unfeeling. He stooped, and began to shuffle some small jagged pieces of ice from one place to another, as though trying to see a pattern in them. There was a terrible sense of futility, of defeat, in his stiff, painful movements. It was as though he had picked up, and rearranged, and set down those same pieces of ice a thousand times before.

"Kai. Talk to me. Tell me what you're trying to do."

He looked up, and at last something stirred behind his clouded pupils.

"It is the Game of Reason," he said. His voice cracked, as though he had not used it for a long time.

Gently, patiently, cradling his icy hands in her own furmittened ones, Gerda asked, "This Game, Kai — does it have a purpose?"

His eyes searched her face, as though there too he sought some pattern he could recognize.

"To spell out a word," he said.

"What word, Kai?"

He gazed down at the ice-puzzle in tired perplexity.

"I don't know," he said. "That is what I must discover. If I can only make the puzzle spell out the right letters, I will comprehend everything, all the knowledge in the world will be mine. This is what the Baroness Aurore has promised me. But I have been re-arranging the pieces for a very long time, and try as I may, I can't make them fit together."

"Shall I try?" asked Gerda.

He gave a hoarse bark of laughter. "You? What can you do? Will you spell out a poem about summer roses?"

"You are cruel," said Gerda, but she spoke without malice. His words had lost their power to wound her. This was not Kai, this creature of ice that the Woman of the North had created in Kai's image.

When she looked down at the shattered surface of the lake, she saw that every broken fragment of ice was like a mirror, and in each one she could see an image of her own face. How strange and ugly those reflections were — her features grotesquely lengthened, flattened, twisted into monstrous shapes. Was this how Kai saw her? Was this how he saw the world, through the distorting lens of the Snow Queen's magic? She thought, *what if after all this ugliness is the true reflection, and everything I have found beautiful in the world is a false image, a foolish lie I have been telling myself?*

And then a sudden gust of wind came shrilling across the ice, so intensely cold that it bit through Gerda's garments of skin and fur and wool, and clawed its way into flesh and bone. She gasped with the ferocity of it; shuddering, she clutched her scarf across her face.

A woman was approaching, gliding swanlike over the frozen lake in a silver-sequined gown. Ice crystals glittered in her loose pale hair, on the shoulders of her ermine cloak. She was tall and slender and beautiful. Her skin was white and delicate as camellia petals, her eyes the glacial blue of sea-ice.

"Well, children, you have found your way at last. Let me congratulate you on your perseverance."

The Snow Queen's voice was as cold as the wind that shrills across the arctic wastes.

"What have you done to Kai?" Sick with anger, Gerda shrieked the question at her.

"Done? I have given him what he wanted most in the world, to look into the Mirror of Reason. And should he succeed in solving my puzzle, then he will know as much as I, and will have nothing more in the world to wish for."

"He will know everything in the world, and feel nothing," Gerda said. She realized as she spoke that she was no longer in awe of this woman, nor afraid of her powers. She had come too far, had survived too much. "You've made a monster of him — a sad, pathetic monster."

In the Snow Queen's eyes there flickered, for an instant, a knowledge as ancient and pitiless as the northern ice. "I made a monster of him? No, my dear child. I think he did that to himself."

"If I can solve the puzzle, then will you let Kai go?"

"You? Let me explain something to you. A hundred philosophers, a hundred men of science have tried and failed to solve my ice-puzzle. What chance could you have of succeeding?"

"But if I do?"

The Snow Queen's laughter, freezing into a cloud of crystals, drifted lazily around them.

"You won't, and I will be bored past endurance watching you try. After a while a game becomes tedious, when you know all the players are bound to lose. So let me propose another kind of game. You fancy yourself a hero, I think, after all your adventures. A hero who has come to free her lover from the sorceress's spell.

"And you —" she turned her chill blue gaze on Ritva — "you are the warrior-shaman, who has come to defeat me, to steal my power from me in my own house."

Ritva stared back at her, unflinching. "I will if I can," she said.

"Well," said the Woman of the North, "if you would play at being heroes, then I will join you in your game. Three impossible tasks to be performed — three challenges. Isn't that how the rules go? You know the fairy tales as well as I."

Gerda glanced at Ritva, who answered with a shrug. Gerda said, "And then can I take Kai home?"

The Snow Queen looked at her with her cold eyes, her thin-lipped, humourless smile. "Home? This is his home now, little Gerda. But if you perform my three tasks, then if he wishes it, I will let him go."

She reached beneath her cloak and drew out a small chased-silver jewel-case. Lifting the lid to show the white velvet lining, she held it out to Gerda. "This is the first and easiest task. You must capture the cold light of a star, and bring it to me in this box."

CHAPTER TWENTY

With that the Snow Queen turned and glided away, her wide skirts making a silken whisper on the marble floors. In the silence that followed, Ritva and Gerda stared at one another.

"You're a shaman's daughter," said Gerda, not very hopefully. "Do you know how to catch a star and put it in a box?"

Ritva snorted. "I heard of a shaman once, who tried to steal the Pole Star, which pins the heavens in place. If he had succeeded, the whole sky would have tumbled down upon the earth."

"That's just a story," Gerda said. "If you tried to fly up above the sky, where the stars are, you would die because there is no air to breathe."

Ritva scratched thoughtfully under the hem of her coat; gazed up at the frosty ceiling; spat.

"Well," said Gerda finally, "if it can't be done with magic, then it must be done with science."

"Science?" said Ritva, looking baffled.

"If I tell you what I mean to do," said Gerda, "you might give the trick away."

"Ah," said Ritva. Her face cleared. "Trickery." She repeated the word, as though relishing the taste of it on her tongue.

❖❖❖

"I have captured a star for you," Gerda told the Snow Queen. She held out the silver box.

"Impossible," said the Baroness Aurore. "Don't waste my time." She waved away the box with an impatient hand.

"No, really. But you must look at it in a dark room, because you can only see stars at night."

"Very well, then," said the Snow Queen. "I suppose I must go along with the joke."

She clapped her hands, and the chandeliers winked out all at once, plunging the room into polar night.

"Watch," said Gerda. In the darkness she could feel Ritva's warm, eager breath on her cheek. She held her own breath, praying that her ruse would work. Slowly, she lifted the lid of the box. Inside on the white velvet nestled a broken arm of her wooden crucifix. It glimmered, as the air reached it, with the cold white luminescence of decay. "Look," murmured Gerda, "you can touch it, it is star-fire, that burns without heat."

"A trick," said the Snow Queen. "Did you think to fool me with a bit of rotting wood?" She clapped her hands again, and the lamps flared up.

"I've brought you what you asked for," said Gerda, calmly. "Cold fire, fox-fire. Star-fire."

"Indeed! And is this how you mean to accomplish all my tasks, by deceit and guile?"

"It's not deceit," said Gerda, meeting the Snow Queen's frigid gaze. "I have done exactly as you asked. I have captured cold fire and put it in a box. And I've practised no more guile than you did, when you ensorcelled Kai."

"Indeed," said the Snow Queen. Her eyes glittered, flat and hard as a serpent's. "Then here is your second task. Let us see if you can accomplish this with your tricks and subterfuges. North of my palace walls is a frozen lake, and beneath the ice swims a silver pike. I fancy that fish for my dinner, and you must catch him for me."

"We have no net," said Ritva.

"Then you must find a way to make one," the Snow Queen said. And she stalked away in a dazzle of spangled silk and diamond-frosted hair.

Gerda turned a glum face to Ritva. "What shall we do? If only we had rescued our fishing gear from the ship . . . "

"If only, if only . . . " mocked Ritva. "If only wishes were fishes, as my mother used to say. If only your Kai had not taken it into his head to run off with a witch . . . There are more ways to catch a fish than with a net," she said. "And more hooks than the ones you stick on the end of a pole. Do you know the story of how the shaman Väinö killed a giant pike with his sword, and made a harp from its jawbones?"

Gerda shook her head.

"Well, that's what he did. And nobody else could play it, but in the shaman's hands all the animals of the forest, all the birds of the air, and all the fish in the rivers came to listen." Her breath puffed out in a white fog as she began to sing, in her hoarse, throaty voice:

All the pikes came swimming,
through the reeds they came to listen,
straightway to the shore they hastened,
there to hear the songs of Väinö . . .

"Come on," she said. "Let's see if we can find any fishbones in the Terrible Enchantress's midden-heap."

Behind the Snow Queen's palace was a winter garden. No green plants grew beside the snowy paths, only trees and fountains and statuary carved from solid ice. Willow trees with silver-frosted trunks and glittering transparent leaves drooped gracefully over frozen streams. Crystal deer, like blown-glass ornaments, grazed on the snowy lawns. At the end of the garden, beyond an orchard of ice-pears hanging like translucent white bells from glassy branches, was a kitchen-midden where all the palace refuse had been thrown. The topmost layer was still fresh and steaming from the midday meal.

Ritva crouched on the frozen ground and began to scrabble though the heap. "Ha!" she said, as she uncovered first the head and then the fleshless spine and tail of an enormous fish. Triumphantly she dragged it out, and began to pick it clean of egg shells and vegetable peelings.

Gerda wrinkled her nose in disgust. "Surely you can't mean to use *that!*"

"Why not? Am I not a shaman, and the daughter of a shaman? What old Väinö could do, I can do." As she worked, Ritva sang cheerfully to herself,

> As he played upon the pike-teeth
> and he lifted up the fish tail
> the horsehair sounded sweetly
> and the horsehair sounded clearly . . .

"We haven't any horsehair," Gerda said.

For answer Ritva pulled off her cap and shook out her mane of black hair, grown lank and long in the months of their journeying. "Here, use my knife," she said.

For an hour or more she squatted patiently at her task, her strong, skilful fingers bending bone and fastening almost invisible hairs with tiny knots. At last, with a satisfied grunt, she held up a strange, misshapen instrument — a fishbone harp.

"Let me hear you play it," said Gerda, through chattering teeth. She felt as though her very bones had turned to ice. If anyone were to touch her, she thought, she would shatter into fragments, like the Snow Queen's mirror.

"Not yet," said Ritva. "First I must sing the rune-magic into it. Then we will go and find this pike, and I will sing the magic out of it again."

It was not a song that Ritva sang, but a queer rising and falling, wailing chant. It was a sound like the storm wind in the forest, like the wolf's howl, and it went on and on, while Gerda shivered and stamped her feet and slapped her arms against her sides.

"I told the harp how I had made it, how we had come to this place, and where I found the bones to fashion it. And now the harp has knowledge of its origins and its true nature, and you will see, though I am no musician, still it will sing sweetly for me."

Ba, who had been lodged all this while in the Snow Queen's stables, looked rested and well-fed. Even his rheumy old eyes seemed brighter as he nuzzled Ritva's neck and thrust his nose inquiringly into Gerda's coat pocket.

"This weather suits you, doesn't it, my poor old bag of bones," said Ritva fondly, as they set out over the trackless white fields. Snow was falling softly through the perpetual silvery half-light of the Snow Queen's kingdom.

The lake spread before them, milk-white and mirror-smooth, fringed by frozen clumps of rushes thrusting up out of a blanket of fresh snow.

Ritva took a rug from Ba's saddlebag, spread it over a flat rock, and sat down on it, her fishbone harp in her hands. The snow had stopped, the air was clear and brittle with cold; the magical lights of the aurora darted and flickered across the sky.

And then the high pure notes rippled forth. In the music of Ritva's harp Gerda could hear all the rainbow colours of the Northern Lights, the sighing of wind, the singing of reeds, the rush and glitter of glacial streams.

On and on Ritva played, in that vast, eternal silence. Beneath the ice Gerda glimpsed a dark shape moving.

Come to me, my great fish,
fish of the broad shoulders and the terrible jaws,
come from the river's cold embrace
to my knife's warm kiss . . .

And suddenly the huge head of the pike burst through the ice. As the harp played on — faster and sweeter, the notes shimmering in the air like pearls, like silver bubbles— a moon-white, silvery-scaled body writhed up through the shattered ice and floundered its way to shore.

The music ended, in a shiver of silvery notes, and in Ritva's hand, now, was the cold gleam of iron.

CHAPTER TWENTY~ONE

"**M**agic," asked the Enchantress of the North, "or more trickery?"

With Ba's help they had dragged the great body of the fish across the snowfields to the palace gates. Now Ritva stood over it, grinning in triumph. "Magic," she said. "This was a wise old fish — not even I could lure him out of his den, except by sorcery."

She plucked a few lively notes on the fishbone harp. Gerda recognized the bawdy soldiers' tune and clapped a hand to her mouth to hide her smile.

"When we've stabled Ba," said Ritva cheerfully, "and you've moved this fish off your doorstep, you can tell us what else you have in mind."

"Is this the third test?"

The Snow Queen's servants had set down an unpainted pinewood chest on the marble tiles of the anteroom. Its sides and curving top were carved with runes.

"I want an embroidered cover for my jewel chest," the Snow Queen said.

"I can do that," said Gerda. "I can do crewel-work, and cross-stitch. And I'm clever at inventing patterns. Give me some silks, and I'll begin at once."

"And where would I find embroidery silks?" asked the Woman of the North. "A good needlewoman supplies her own. No, these are the things you must stitch into your work — the purple of the lichen that grows on the stones beside the River of the Dead; a white swan's feather floating on that river; and the blood-red of the berries that grow at the entrance to the Dead Land. With these colours you must dye your yarns; your spindle and distaff and needle you must fashion for yourself."

Beyond the Snow Queen's palace lay the hidden path to the Dead Land: a path that twisted and coiled its tortuous way downward through sunless gorges, wreathed in mist.

As the road steadily descended, the air grew milder and more humid. Now patches of grey earth, dead grass and broken stone showed through the snow. Still further, the snow had all but disappeared, leaving hummocks of sodden, spongy ground rising out of black meltwater pools. The clean, biting cold of the snowfields gave way to a damp grey chill that crept into the bones.

Jagged black boulders, their fissures and crevices rimed with hoarfrost, guarded the shores of the river that circled the Dead Land. A thick grey mist hid the farther bank. Everything was lifeless, colourless: black oily water, dull black stone, grey earth under a pewter sky. The only sound was the hungry suck and slap of the river as it washed upon the rocks.

"This is a terrible place," Gerda whispered. There was a heavy, dragging feeling around her heart. Every emotion seemed to have been drained out of her; she was beyond terror, or horror, or despair. Nothing mattered, now. Why had she imagined she could rescue Kai? Why had she imagined Kai would want to be rescued? She would lie down on the black stones of the river shore, and let sleep overtake her.

She felt Ritva shaking her, so hard that her head rocked back on her shoulders. Pain lanced through her tongue as a tooth bit into it. She spat blood.

She leaned against Ritva, looking sadly at the bright splatter of crimson — the only patch of colour in this dreary place.

"Don't give up on me now," snarled Ritva. "You started all this — now help me finish it."

The pain in her mouth made Gerda angry, and the anger cleared her head a little. Irritably, she pushed Ritva away. "The lichen," she said. "Where is the lichen? Help me look among the rocks."

They searched for a long time, finding only rotting snow and stone rubble. "Let Ba smell it out," Ritva said, untying the old beast's rope. Freed from his tether, the reindeer thrust a curious nose into the shadowy crevice between two tall pillars of rock. Crouching on her heels, Gerda dug her fingers cautiously into the crack, and pried loose a brittle, crumbling handful of grey-green moss.

She held it out to Ritva, who sniffed it, and tasted a bit of it on the end of her tongue, and finally put it away in her pack.

"Now for the white swan's feather," Ritva said, and she sat down on a flat rock with her harp.

Ritva's hands flew over the strings and notes tumbled forth like bright beads of water. "Come to me," she whispered, her fingers dancing. The music swelled, cascaded. And presently, gliding out of the grey mist that hid the entrance to the underworld, came three white swans.

Nearer and nearer they drifted, pale, glimmering shapes in the grey half-light. Ritva began to sing, a deep-throated wordless summoning. And then she reached out— slowly, gently — and plucked a single feather from the first swan's breast.

She turned, and smiled, and laid the feather in Gerda's outstretched hand as gallantly as a soldier presenting a trophy to his queen.

But one more task remained. Across the cold grey river, at the gates of the Dead Kingdom, grew the berries whose blood-red colour Gerda must stitch into her pattern. And those berries seemed to Gerda as hopelessly out of reach as if they were growing a world away in her mother's kitchen-garden.

"The last task is always the hardest," Ritva said, with gloomy resignation, and she began to unfasten her heavy wolfskin coat. Slowly she peeled off her cap, her boots, her leather tunic, a ragged sweater or two, her reindeer-skin breeches and the tattered woollen undervest she had stolen from a seaman.

"No, Ritva, you must not," cried Gerda, when she realized what the robber-maid meant to do. "The water is too cold, too deep. Look out there in the middle, how fast the current runs."

"I've swum in colder rivers than this," said Ritva. "Stop chattering, and I'll fetch these accursed berries for you." She took a length of cord from Ba's saddle-pack and and tied a draw-string pouch around her waist. "Take care of my harp," she said, putting the awkward instrument into Gerda's hands. "And Ba."

Shivering in the damp, raw air, she scrambled down the bank to the river's edge, and waded straight out into the current, as calmly as if she were stepping into a warm bath.

The water foamed and boiled around her — thigh, waist, shoulder high. For a moment or two her head bobbed upon the surface; then, as Gerda watched in horror, the river swept her up and she was gone.

Gerda's stomach clenched; panic, sour and choking, flooded her chest. Ritva is drowned for sure, she thought. I have let her do this for my sake, and now I will never see her again. Sick with fear — for Ritva, for herself — she prayed aloud, to the indifferent sky, and the silent, watchful stones: *Only let her reach the other side, and return safe, and I will never lead her into danger again.* She was not sure, at that moment, if she prayed to her own Christian God, or to the strange wild deities that haunted Ritva's world.

Endless moments passed. The river churned and eddied; mist-wraiths swirled above the other, hidden shore.

And then a dark head, wet and sleek as an otter's, broke though the surface.

Ritva swam to shore, breasting the current with powerful, steady strokes. Scowling and spitting out water, she clambered up onto the bank. The deerskin pouch hung sodden and heavy against her hip.

She tried to untie the cord, but was shivering so violently that her fingers would not obey her. "Take it," she told Gerda through chattering teeth.

Gerda undid the knot, retrieved the bulging pouch and loosened its string. She peered inside. "You brought back the berries!"

"Well, didn't I say I would?" Ritva's jaw was clattering so hard that she could scarcely speak. "Now hand me my clothes, before I finish freezing to death."

"How shall I stitch a fanciwork cover, with no needle, and without any silks?" sighed Gerda. "And as to the rest . . . " She gathered up the reindeer moss, the red berries, the white swan's feather, and held them out to Ritva. "What am I supposed to do with these?"

"We boil them," said Ritva, and she set off to the Snow Queen's kitchen in search of a kettle.

The Snow Queen's kitchen was a bleak, unwelcoming place. The floor was made of milky-white marble, the walls of glazed white tiles. Even the oven bricks were made of some glittery white stone. Gerda thought wistfully of her mother's bright kitchen with its cheerful curtains and embroidered chair covers, its painted crockery and enticing smells of spice and coffee and fresh-baked bread. Still, this was the warmest spot in the Snow Queen's palace, and Gerda huddled gratefully by the tall white porcelain-tiled stove, in which a low fire burned. Ritva, meanwhile, had dumped the handful of lichen into a pot, and retreated with it into the pantry. When she returned, she set the pot on the warm hob. Before long a sharp smell of ammonia filled the room.

"What stinks?" asked Gerda, with her hand over her nose.

"Never mind that," said Ritva. "I'm making dye for your embroidery thread."

"And what do we do now?"

"Now we leave it to ferment."

She dumped the red berries into another pot, added water from the hearth-kettle, poked up the cooking fire, and set the pot to boil.

Then she opened the kitchen door and whistled to the great white wolf-dog who slept in a kennel just outside. He came to her at once, wriggling like a pup on his belly, tail thumping, tongue lolling, rubbing his huge white muzzle against her sleeve. "Nice dog, good dog," muttered Ritva absently, as she combed her fingers through his long, thick hair.

"There's your embroidery silk," she said, holding up handfuls of soft white undercoat.

"And how shall I turn it into yarn, without a spinning wheel?"

"What, should poor old Ba have carried a spinning wheel across the ice on his back?" asked Ritva. "My mother's people have no spinning wheels. Watch, and I'll show you how it's done."

She picked up a loose clump of dog hair, drew it out and flattened it and wound it round her right hand. Tucking her tunic tightly under her thighs, she held the end of the hank in her left hand, while her right hand, moving adroitly up and down, rolled the hairs into a single thread across her knee. She wound the finished strand slowly around three fingers, holding it taut with thumb and forefinger, and eventually held up for Gerda's inspection a length of coarse, lumpy white yarn.

Gerda looked dubiously at it. "It's awfully thick," she said. "And I still need a piece of canvas and a needle."

"You must make do with reindeer skin," Ritva told her. "And I'll carve you a needle out of bone. But you must draw the pattern."

Gerda sat pondering this with her back pressed up against the stove. "Roses," she said finally. "I'll make a pattern of roses, like the ones on our rooftop garden. And when Kai sees it, maybe it will remind him of home."

The lichen had fermented into a violet-coloured soup; the stewed berries sat in a dark crimson juice. Ritva dipped one length of yarn into the lichen dye, and the other into the berry juice. The colours, when she held them up to admire them, were deep and rich.

"They're lovely," said Gerda, and resolutely set to work.

The cold made her fingers so stiff and clumsy she could scarcely grip her needle. Every stitch through the tough rein-deer hide was a painful effort, and before long tears of frustra-tion were rolling down her cheeks. After a while her hands grew so numb that they no longer seemed attached to her wrists. She got up, flapped her arms and stamped her feet to keep the blood flowing, wiped her eyes on her sleeve, and took up her stitchery again.

Over and over, with fierce determination, she forced the blunt bone needle through the hide. For my sake, she told herself, Ritva risked her life in the icy currents of the river. Though my fingers freeze, though my blood turns to ice in my veins, I will not complain about this simple seamstress's task.

At last the cover was finished. Once Gerda would have been ashamed to show anyone such crude, clumsy work; she would have picked out all the threads and begun again. But now she examined with unexpected pride the big, uneven stitches, the lumpy crimson roses with their strange violet-coloured leaves. The task was meant to be impossible — and together she and Ritva had found a way to do it.

Chapter Twenty~two

"We've completed every one of your tasks," Gerda said. "We've earned Kai's freedom. Now you must let him go." But her courage wavered as she met the Snow Queen's cold, implacable gaze.

"And who are you to tell me what I must do? In my own time, I will give Kai his freedom."

"But you promised!" Gerda's voice was shrill with indignation.

"What did I promise? To play a game. Did I say there would be a prize for winning?"

"But you said . . . " Gerda subsided into outraged silence. A bargain had been struck, and they had kept their side of it. She could find no words to protest such injustice, such shameless betrayal.

"I said nothing. I can hardly be blamed if you choose to make assumptions. All these tricks of yours have been entertaining — but the price for Kai comes higher than that."

Ritva asked, in a hoarse, flat voice, "What *is* the price then?"

"You're asking me to make a sacrifice," the Snow Queen said. "I've grown fond of your friend Kai: he is clever, and amusing. So I will ask a sacrifice in return. If you would earn his freedom, you must do as the people of the northlands do — you must give up your most precious possession."

"Then the price is nothing at all," said Gerda, "for we have nothing to give up."

"Ah, but you're wrong," the Snow Queen said. "When the people of the northlands ask a favour from their gods, they understand the price. They know they must offer up the life of their best animal. Their favourite dog. The strongest reindeer in the herd."

Behind her, Gerda heard the sudden rasping intake of Ritva's breath.

"Not Ba," Gerda whispered. "You would not ask us to kill Ba."

The Snow Queen smiled. "If you would rob me of Kai, then you must pay the penalty."

"No! Ritva, you must not!"

"You want your Kai, don't you?" said Ritva. Her voice sounded choked and strange. "Isn't that why we came here?"

Fiercely, she wrapped her arms around the old reindeer's grizzled neck. When she looked up Gerda saw that the robber-maid's mouth was trembling, and her eyes were blurred with tears. Something sharp and painful twisted in Gerda's chest. It was the first time that she had ever seen Ritva weep.

"Not if Ba must die for it. Nothing is worth that price."

"It's what my mother's ancestors did. What their gods demanded of them."

Gerda put her own arms around Ritva — cautiously, for fear of being rebuffed. The old reindeer turned his head to peer curiously at them both. "The Snow Queen is not a god, she's just a vile, treacherous woman. And anyway, if she broke her other promise, why wouldn't she break this one as well?"

"Do you mean it — you would give up Kai to save Ba?"

Gerda drew a long, slow breath. Was this the choice she must make? Must she sacrifice Kai, and her dreams of a future with Kai, so that Ba could live?

She took Ritva's cold, trembling hands in her own.

"Don't you see what she wants, Ritva? How cruel and calculating she is, to give us a choice that must tear the two of us apart?"

"But you love Kai . . . "

"And you love Ba. Surely, Ritva, the two of us together can outwit her. She does not deserve to win."

Ritva picked up the fishbone harp and settled it on her knees. Her fingers drifted across the strings, coaxing forth a sweet, slumbrous music. In those languid notes, Gerda could hear the rippling of water among green reeds, the wind in the yellow grass of August, the murmuring of bees on summer air. Her eyelids drooped; her limbs felt slack and heavy.

And then she was sitting high up over a cobbled street, with the hot sun beating down on her shoulders. She was dressed in white muslin, with pink ribbons in her hair, and the air was filled with the scent of roses.

"Wake up! Wake up!" In the midst of her dream, rough hands were shaking her, slapping her cheeks. But she must not wake up. If she clung to sleep she could stay in this warm, summer place forever. *Go away*, she wanted to shout. *Leave me alone*. But no sound came from her lips. She tried to strike out at those infuriating hands, but her arms hung inert as blocks of wood. Someone prodded her in the ribs, yanked savagely on her hair. Gerda's eyes flew open, and she let out a protesting shriek as the dream shattered and cold reality rushed in.

Ritva's hands were on Gerda's shoulders, still shaking her. She let go, and grinned.

"Not you, you stupid thing, I didn't mean *you* to go to sleep!"

Gerda peered groggily about her. She saw two kitchen servants slumped beside the hearth, their snores rattling around the big white-tiled room. The guard dog slept with his nose on his paws, and the cook dozed sitting up with a ladle in her hand.

"They're all asleep," said Ritva happily. "All over the palace. Even the Snow Queen. I've charmed them all to sleep with my music. See —" She prodded the cook with her foot. The woman made a grumbling noise in her throat and toppled gently sideways till her head came to rest on a sack of flour.

Gerda stood up, feeling dazed and lightheaded. She put her hand over her mouth to stifle a yawn.

"We must find Kai," she said.

In all that frozen palace, only Kai was awake. He was huddled, as always, in the midst of the Mirror of Reason, intent on shifting ice-fragments into ever-changing patterns. But the fragments were smaller now, mere shards and splinters, as though he no longer had the strength to drag the heavier pieces from place to place. His listless, repetitive movements slowed as Gerda and Ritva approached, but he did not look up.

"Kai!" Gerda leaned down. The words came out in a hoarse whisper. "Come with us, Kai. We are going home."

Gaunt, grey, hollow-eyed, he turned his face to her. She wanted to weep for the deep lines across his forehead, the shadows under his eyes.

"You can't go home," he said in a dull, hopeless voice. "No one leaves this place. There is no way out."

"Have you ever tried to leave?"

He shook his head. "What would be the point? Someday I will solve the ice puzzle, and everything I have been promised will be mine. And what are the alternatives? To be killed by the hounds that guard the gates, or to freeze to death in the snow?"

"Kai," Gerda said softly. She picked up a piece of ice in her mittened hands and held it to his face. "Look at yourself, Kai. Look hard and tell me what you see."

His gaze slid away, stared into the white distance. "Look," she said, with stubborn patience. "You are already frozen half to death."

At last he looked into the mirror. Gerda, head close to his, looked with him, and saw that the ice mirror showed his true image: the worn, wind-chapped, haggard features, the eyes glazed with suffering and exhaustion, the flesh worn to the bone.

"This is the Snow Queen's gift," said Gerda. "She has given you a riddle with no answer, and she will keep you here until your soul is frozen into a lump of ice."

Kai said, with childlike persistence, "But I have not solved the puzzle. I must spell out the answer to the Snow Queen's riddle, and then I will know everything there is to know in the world."

"You cannot know everything in the world," said Gerda sadly. "Only God and his angels know that." How strange that she should say these things to Kai — he had always been the one who talked, and she the one who listened. Yet at this moment she felt years older than Kai, and immeasurably wiser.

"She has deceived you, Kai. Everything she told you was a trick and a deception. We have come to take you home, to the people who love you and are waiting for you."

"No one leaves here without her permission," Kai said in a dreary monotone, as though he were repeating a formula by rote. For answer, Gerda seized his hands, and dragged him to his feet.

"Nonsense," she said. "We need no one's permission. Show him what you've done, Ritva." She took firm hold of Kai's arm and led him, weakly protesting, to the edge of the frozen lake. Together they followed Ritva through the echoing icy corridors, the vaulted moon-white rooms of the Snow Queen's palace. Everywhere was emptiness and silence.

"Where are her guards, her servants, her dogs?" Kai whispered.

"I played them a lullaby on my fishbone harp," said Ritva. Her eyes danced with mischief, and delight in her own cleverness. "The cooks are asleep in the kitchen, and the guards are asleep in the guardroom. The dogs are snoring beside the gates."

"Where is the rune-chest?" Kai asked. "We must take it with us."

"What, that heavy thing?" said Ritva "What use is it? We have enough to carry."

For an instant something hard and dangerous blazed in Kai's eyes. When he answered Ritva, it was in a cool, patronizing tone that Gerda recognized all too well. "Don't you understand? We can't leave the chest behind. It's the source of all her power."

"What's in it?" Ritva wanted to know. She sounded skeptical, but interested.

"No one knows that. It is never opened."

"You mean there is magic in it?" persisted Ritva.

"Only if by magic, you mean the secret patterns of the universe. One day, she promised, she would unlock the box and reveal its contents to me."

"And now you mean to steal it."

Kai's grey features flushed with sudden anger. "It is mine by right," he said. "Haven't I earned it, all these weary months, shuffling and reshuffling the ice pieces, looking for an answer you tell me I was never meant to find?"

Ritva shrugged. "Fetch the chest," she said. "And bring some rope, for you must carry it on your own back. My poor old beast has enough to do."

Stepping around the sleeping hounds, they went out into the starlit night. The air was clear, the snow frozen into a crust as smooth and hard as pavement.

Ba's saddlebags were full again, with provisions hastily collected from the palace larder.

At first Kai insisted on carrying the Snow Queen's treasure chest clutched awkwardly to his chest, but after a few steps he faltered, his knees buckling under him.

"It's too heavy for him, we must let Ba carry it," pleaded Gerda.

But Kai was as stubborn as Ritva. "Give me that length of rope —I'll drag it behind me," he muttered, and he plodded dourly onward with the rope over his shoulder, the chest in its bright needlework cover trailing after him like an obstinate hound on a leash.

"How do you know the way?" Gerda asked Ritva, as she hurried to keep up with the robber-maid's brisk, confident stride.

Ritva turned, and grinned. "While you were dreaming, I also dreamed," she said. "I sent my spirit southward, to chart our path. And I saw something else in my vision, little rabbit. At the sea's edge, I saw a fine, large boat, just waiting for somebody like us to steal it."

Before long Kai's pace began to flag and he fell behind. "Wait," said Gerda, running to catch up with the robber-maid. "We must go slower; Kai is too ill to keep up."

Ritva turned, and with a contemptuous glance at Kai said, "Then tell him we'll leave him to find his own way home."

Gerda gasped. "Ritva, you can't mean it!"

"Do you think the Snow Queen's guards will sleep forever? Even now they must be yawning and stirring. Our only chance is to reach the open sea."

Gerda looked back. Kai was trudging doggedly after them, but he walked like an old man, halt and bent.

Gerda ran back to him, seized his arm. He gave her a despairing look. "It's no use," he said. "You must leave me, and save yourself."

"Don't be ridiculous," said Gerda, in the firm governess's voice her mother sometimes used. "You must lean on me, and we will walk together."

They stumbled onward over glittering white plains lit feverishly by the northern lights.

In this kingdom beyond the world's edge, time and distance behaved in unpredictable ways. Only a few hours had passed when they came again to the edge of the ice, and saw a wide channel of open water stretching away south. Drawn up on the ice, just as Ritva had said, was a wide flat-bottomed skin boat with a set of paddles stowed inside. The three of them pushed it into the dark choppy water. Gerda braced her feet on the ice and held onto the painter while Ritva coaxed Ba on board.

Ba, who had shied at first sight of the boat, flung up his grizzled head, stiffening all four legs and digging his hooves into the snow.

Ritva whispered into his ear, "Get moving, you poor old bag of bones, if you ever want to see your own pasture again," and grudgingly he let her lead him on board.

"How are we to find our way home?" asked Gerda, looking out over the dark, wind-torn water. Beside her, Kai was a silent, huddled presence. She wanted to put her arms around him, warm his cold, gaunt cheek against hers, but so much a stranger had he become, so wrapped in his own grim solitude, that she did not dare to touch him.

"Home is south," said Ritva, adding, with inarguable logic, "from here, every direction is south, so whichever direction we go, we will be headed home. We must trust to chance."

Or to God, thought Gerda, but she did not say it aloud.

"Here," said Ritva, thrusting a paddle at Kai. "You sit in the back and steer."

A wind blew up out of the north, and sped them on their way. They must have chanced upon a warm current, because there was open water ahead — a broad ice-free channel like a high road leading south. Gerda's spirits rose. Perhaps, after all, God had heard her, and was taking their fate into His own hands.

She helped Ritva put up the boat's small triangular sail, and they let the wind and current propel them. After a while Gerda fell into a half-doze, a kind of waking dream. She thought that she was at home, and that she was helping her mother hang the bedcovers out to air. But there was a storm coming; the wind bellied out the quilts and made them flap on the line, with a sound like the beating of wings.

Cold and damp, finding its way under her fur garments, woke her. All around them a dense silvery fog swirled and billowed. She could see neither sky, nor water, nor the icefields beyond.

The wind had freshened, filling their sail, and they were moving quickly, but in what direction it was impossible to tell.

Suddenly the mist parted, and out of it emerged a great broad-beamed wooden ship with a single square sail. It had come so silently out of the fog that now it was almost upon them. Gerda could see the rapid lift and fall of oars along the sides, the skin-clad warriors lining the deck, and the tall woman in white furs standing in the bow with her pale hair swirling about her.

Swiftly the Snow Queen's ship bore down upon them, the north wind swelling out its sail. Ritva and Gerda paddled furiously, but with every stroke they were losing ground.

"It's the chest," Kai told them. "All her power is in it, and she will follow it to the far ends of the earth to get it back."

"The bag of winds," shouted Gerda, leaning hard into her stroke. "Open the bag of winds."

Ritva fumbled for the pouch. It hung from her fingers, limp and spent. "It's empty," Gerda said.

"No. There are two more knots." Ritva pulled off her mitts and with cold, stiff fingers she worried at the knots till she had worked both of them loose. There was a sighing, a hissing, a roar, and Ritva fell backwards with a thump as the winds rushed out. With the force of an arctic gale they battered the Snow Queen's warship, heeled it over, spun it round.

"Paddle," shrieked Ritva, picking herself up. "Just keep paddling, don't turn around."

But Kai, crouched in the stern, looked back; and moments later, with bleak resignation, he said, "The winds have died down. She is gaining on us again."

Ritva glanced over her shoulder, and mumbled something in Saami. "Here, you, come forward and take over." Gingerly she and Kai changed places.

Ritva turned to Gerda. "Do you still have our flint and tinder in your pocket?"

Gerda nodded. For one wild moment she imagined that Ritva intended to set them all afire. "Why?"

"Give it to me. Am I not the daughter of shamans? Have I not accomplished every task the Snow Queen gave me? Have I not stolen her treasure chest from under her nose? I am a hero, like Väinö. What Väinö could do, I can do also."

She snatched up a handful of the dried moss they used for tinder, crunched it into a ball, and threw it over the stern. And lacking her drum, she used her right hand to pound out a rhythm on the boat's taut skin hull. Her voice rose, fell, rose again in an eerie wail. Her arm and hand kept up their rhythmic motion, beating out her shaman's tattoo. The rest of her body was rigid, every muscle quivering with tension. Veins bulged in her temples; her lower lip sagged and foam gathered in the corners of her mouth. Her eyes stared blindly into the fog.

The clump of moss bobbed for a moment on the black surface of the water — and then, spongelike, it began to swell. Now it was as big as a bread loaf; now the size of a cheese. As Gerda and Kai stared in delighted disbelief, and Ritva kept up her monotonous drumming, the tinder continued, improbably, to grow. Where there had been open water there was now a great, dark, mossy reef that blocked the whole width of the channel. On one side was their heavy-laden, lumbering skin boat; on the other, the Snow Queen's swiftly-moving warship.

They could hear shouting, the splash of oars, the creak of timbers; a sound of slithering and crunching; and then the bow of the Snow Queen's vessel ploughed its way straight through the reef.

"Now give me the flint. And keep paddling. I'll stop her yet." Ritva drew a long, deep, rasping breath, and once again began to beat on the side of the boat. As she drummed she muttered and mumbled to herself, sometimes singing a few incomprehensible syllables. Her eyes were shuttered, remote. A thread of saliva worked its way slowly down her chin.

Then she drew back her arm and with all her remaining strength hurled the fragment of flint over the stern. At the instant it struck the water, the flint began to grow.

For years afterwards Gerda was to dream of the wall of glistening grey-black stone that suddenly and impossibly, like a mountain newborn from the sea's bed, thrust itself out of the depths. At that moment, for the first time, she glimpsed the true nature of Ritva's power. This was no illusion, no conjurer's trick, but real stone, solid and impenetrable, created out of a bit of flint, and air, and sea-spume. *Truly*, thought Gerda, *Ritva is the heir of the magical smith Ilmarinen in the old tales, who forged a new sun and a new moon for the heavens, and welded the arch of air.*

And now the Snow Queen's ship was trapped behind the mountain Ritva had forged, and after all it seemed they might escape.

Out of the mist that wreathed the clifftop flew a huge white bird, its silvery wing tips gleaming in the starlight. It hovered for an instant on powerful wings, then dove down upon their boat like an eagle swooping at its prey. They could see the malevolent glitter of ice-blue eyes, talons pale and glimmering as shards of ice.

Ba's eyes bulged with terror; he flung his head wildly from side to side. A pale, exhausted Ritva seized his rope and whispered in his ear to calm him.

Standing upright in the rocking boat, Gerda flailed at the bird with her paddle. The creature flew so close that its icy wing tips brushed her face; then, as though taunting her, it darted out of reach. Gerda fought to keep her balance. Her arm and shoulder muscles shrieked with pain.

Just then Ritva, savagely swinging her own paddle, landed a heavy blow. Squawking and screeching, one wing drooping, the white bird fluttered away. It hung in the air a paddle's length off, glaring at them.

"The chest," Ritva hissed to Gerda. "It's the chest she wants; her magic is in it."

"No! The chest is mine!"

Gerda closed her ears to Kai's anguished protest. She dropped her paddle and reached into the bottom of the boat. Lifting the chest over her head, she flung it as far as she could over the side. But just then the boat lurched in the wind, and her aim went wrong. Instead of falling into the water the chest struck the base of the flint cliff. The wood splintered and the decorated lid flew off, scattering ice fragments like diamonds across the wet black rock. One by one they slipped down the face of the cliff into the sea.

With a shriek of fury the great white bird dove down, snatched up in its beak a single shard of ice, and flew away with it.

Ritva gave a long sigh and sank down in the bottom of the boat.

"Look," cried Gerda.

On the dark surface of the water, the ice fragments were shifting and bobbing among the splintered remains of the chest. Bit by bit they came together, made a pattern. Silently Gerda's lips formed the single word the ice spelled out.

Was it just another riddle, Gerda wondered — a cruel trick by a sorceress who had only riddles to offer, and no answers? Or was it the answer to a question that Kai had never asked? She took his icy fingers in her right hand, and with her left she pointed to the shimmering ice-characters that danced on the dark skin of the sea.

"Remember, the Snow Queen said that if you solved the puzzle, you would comprehend everything, all knowledge would be yours. But you did not ask how long it would take you, Kai."

One letter a time, in a cracked, hoarse voice that seemed wrenched from somewhere deep in his soul, Kai spelled out the word that he had laboured so long to discover:

E.T.E.R.N.I.T.Y.

Gerda saw his face twist into a mask of rage. Leaning over the stern, he shouted into the teeth of the north wind, "Witch, have you no mercy? You have tricked me again!"

His words were swallowed up in the infinite grey air, in the eternal restless music of the sea.

How many others before him, wondered Gerda, had discovered too late the capriciousness of the Snow Queen's favours? How many had forfeited their souls because they listened to her promises?

But hearing the fury and despair, the naked anguish in Kai's voice, Gerda thought, *at last the frozen shell around his heart is melting, he is remembering how to feel pain.*

Their boat sped on, steadily southward. They passed through the Cave of the North Wind, out of winter and night, into the long bright arctic summer. The sun glared down on dazzling icefields that parted to let them through.

And in the southern distance they saw a glimmer of white sails.

Chapter Twenty-three

The *Northwind* was a sturdy two-masted schooner, her hull planked all over with oak timbers and her bows iron-sheathed to withstand the Arctic ice.

"Ahoy," someone shouted in Swedish over the side. "Do you need help?"

"Yes! Yes!" They hurled their joined voices into the wind.

"Come alongside," said the sailor, and flung a rope ladder over the rail.

"Our reindeer," Gerda called up to them as Ritva steered their boat towards the ship. "We have to rescue our reindeer."

A red-bearded man in a parka grinned down at them. "We're scientists here," he said. "Hold on. We'll think of something."

Moments later he returned with a canvas sling and dropped it down to them. Bracing themselves against Ba's heaving flanks, Gerda and Ritva cinched the sling securely around his belly. With a long unhappy sigh the old beast resigned himself to this fresh indignity, gazing accusingly back at them as he was winched slowly up the side of the ship.

With Ba safely on deck, Gerda, Ritva and Kai clambered aboard.

Immediately someone threw woollen blankets over their shoulders; someone else handed them steaming mugs of coffee, laced with spirits and tasting of salt.

The red-bearded man introduced himself as Otto Carlsson, the Assistant Navigator. He took them into the cabin and sat them down in front of a blazing coal stove, then watched with a mixture of amusement and concern as they worked their way through a huge meal of rye bread, walrus meat, salt fish and stewed apples. At length he leaned back in his chair with a fresh mug of coffee and said, "What in Heaven's name are you doing adrift in these waters? Were you shipwrecked?"

Stupefied by exhaustion, the fire's warmth, the hot food in her stomach, Gerda could, for once in her life, think of no convincing lie. And if she were to tell this rational-minded man of science the truth, how could she expect him to believe her? It was Kai, finally, who spoke up.

"We were with a geographic expedition from the University of Uppsala, exploring the west coast of Novaya Zemlya. But foolishly we became separated from our ship, lost our bearings, and were swept out to sea."

"Foolish indeed," said Carlsson. "You are fortunate to have survived. But I fear we cannot help you to rejoin your ship. Like yourselves, we have been engaged in geographic studies, charting the coast of Spitzbergen. But now we are homeward bound to Gothenburg by way of Vardö."

"But we don't want to go back to our ship," said Gerda sleepily. "By now our colleagues will have sailed without us, believing us to have perished. Kai and I must return at once to Copenhagen, to let our families know that we are safe."

"Then once again you're in luck," said Carlsson. "Our chief cartographer is Danish, and I'm sure he'll be pleased to escort you safely back to Copenhagen."

Gerda thought happily of Copenhagen — soft towels, white sheets, clean clothes, and then a carriage to take her home. The voices around her faded to a pleasant blur.

And then she felt someone tugging urgently at her sleeve. She looked round to see a scowling Ritva.

"Come here." The robber-maid dragged Gerda around a bulkhead, out of earshot of the crew. "What is this man saying to you?"

"Why," said Gerda drowsily, "that they will see Kai and me safely home to Denmark. We have been a long time absent, Ritva, and our families will have given us up for dead. Think how happy they will be when I return, and bring Kai with me."

"And me?"

In the robber-maid's dark eyes, for a fleeting moment, there was a look of wistfulness, of yearning.

"Ritva, if you wish they will take you back to the coast of Finland, and from there you can make your way to your father's camp."

Ritva's face suddenly hardened, became heavy and sullen. "Why would I go back to that place? There is nothing for me there."

"Your mother is there. Surely in her own way she must care about you."

Furiously, Ritva shook her head. Gerda was startled to see that her eyes glistened with tears. In a gruff voice Ritva said, "And what will you do when you get home? Will you marry *him*?" She jerked her head towards Kai with undisguised contempt.

Gerda felt the blood rushing to her face. Stammering, she said, "Why . . . yes, if he'll have me . . . that's what we always planned . . . "

"And that will make you happy? Scrubbing the floor and mending his shirts and wiping the noses of his brats?"

"It's what we've always planned . . . " Gerda repeated, help-lessly.

But what were Kai's plans, now? At this moment he was hunched over a table with the chief cartographer, watching him draw up new charts of the Spitzbergen coastline. And she realised that Kai had spoken scarcely three words to her since their rescue.

Ritva stared over the rail into the ice-flecked, sunlit sea. She quoted, with bitter sarcasm,

A maiden's life is bright as a day in summer,
a wife's lot is colder than the frost.
A maiden is as free as the berries in the forest
a wife is like a dog tied up with a rope.

"That's horrible," said Gerda. "Don't you ever mean to marry?"

"Me? Not a chance. Can you see me darning trousers, and stirring the stewpot? I am a shaman, little rabbit. I am a woman of power. I have travelled to the spirit kingdom. I have defeated the Dark Enchantress, and brought you safely back from beyond the world's edge."

"A woman of power," repeated Gerda, liking the sound of those words.

"As you are too, little rabbit," said Ritva, surprisingly. "It was you who saved Kai's life. And see how grateful he is, how he gets down on his knees to thank the hero who rescued him."

At once, Gerda leaped to Kai's defense. "It's only that the Snow Queen has put a spell upon him. You'll see, Ritva, now that he has escaped from her clutches, he will soon be his old self again."

"And what was that like, his old self? Was that the one the Snow Queen stole from him?"

"Oh, Ritva, if you could have known him then — he was clever, and witty, and brave, and I loved him . . . "

"So it seems," said Ritva wryly. "To follow him to the world's end. And Kai? Did he love you as much as that? If the Snow Queen had stolen you, little rabbit, would your Kai have set out across the frozen seas to save you?"

Gerda stared at the robber-maid in stricken silence. *Oh, yes,* she wanted desperately to say. *He was my dearest friend. Of course he would have saved me.* But the words stuck in her throat. With Ritva's sardonic gaze upon her, all she could utter was the sad, inadequate truth.

"Oh, Ritva, do not ask me that, for I cannot answer."

"Then ask him."

"Ritva, don't be absurd, I could never do such a thing."

"I could," said Ritva, turning purposefully in Kai's direction.

"No!" cried Gerda, horrified.

Ritva waited.

"Oh, very well," said Gerda. "Of course I will not ask him that, but it will do no harm to speak to him." She marched resolutely across the deck. "Kai," she said, standing at his shoulder. "Kai . . . "

He glanced up in polite inquiry, his forefinger marking his place. There was colour in his cheeks now, and his eyes were clear and alert. But where, in that thin, worn stranger's face, was the friend of her childhood, the kind, clever boy for whom she had dared so much?

Had the Snow Queen stolen Kai's true self — or had he simply lost it somewhere, laid it aside and forgotten it like a cap or a half-read book?

And the thought came to her, like cold fingers clutching her heart — if you lose your self, can you ever find it again?

Kai gave her a slightly abstracted smile. "Can we talk a little later, Gerda, when I've finished with this?"

She bit her lip. "It was nothing, Kai," she said, as she turned away. "Nothing that cannot wait."

"And what will you do, now — you and Ba?"

Ritva gave Gerda a sly look. "Maybe we will ride south one day, and visit you in your rose garden."

"Would you? Truly?" For one moment Gerda had an image of Ritva sitting in her boots and ragged tunic in the Jensen parlour, drinking coffee and eating ginger-cakes from the best porcelain, while Ba, with a wreath of roses round his antlers, munched on carrots. She clapped a hand over her mouth to hide her smile.

"Why not? But first I am going to pay another visit to the old woman who writes on codfish, and the old woman who binds the winds. Maybe they have other things to teach me."

Gerda thought of the unlooked-for joy, the rapturous light-ness of spirit she had felt on their autumn journey across the empty northern lands. She remembered the thrill of triumph that had come in the midst of cold and despair, when she and the robber-maid, standing fast together, pitted their skills against the Snow Queen's magic.

She remembered the sun glinting on arctic seas the colour of emeralds, of aquamarine, and the wild flare of the northern lights across a starlit sky.

She had been to the farthermost edge of the world, where earth and day end. There was no road, now, that she would be afraid to travel. How could she be content to dream away her life in a southern rose garden?

Gerda leaned forward, put her arms around Ritva's shoul-ders, pressed her own chapped, windburned cheek against the robber-maid's.

"Come soon, dear friend," she whispered. "While the roads to the north are clear. I will be waiting."